SPENCER COHEN, BOOK ONE

THE SPENCER COHEN SERIES

N.R. WALKER

COPYRIGHT

DEDICATION

This series is dedicated to every Spencer out there: for those who have lost everything but still have hope, for those too afraid to love again but crave it all the same, for those who have been through hell yet are still strong enough to smile, and for those who wear their scars inked into their skin.

N.R. WALKER

THE SPENCER COHEN

SERIES BOOK ONE

ONE

I walked out of the tattoo shop on Abbot Kinney Boulevard and smiled into the warm LA afternoon sun. My last job had paid well, so I'd just put two month's rent in my landlord's hand for the small apartment above the shop that I'd called home since I'd arrived from Australia two years ago.

I loved this place. Los freakin' Angeles. I fit in here. I found the one place where I could be me, where I belonged. There was always bustling, always something doing. A million strangers, yet I'd come to know the locals and some of them even called me by name.

"Hey, Spencer!"

Lola waved at me from a table at the back of the coffee shop. She looked gorgeous, as always. Her usual 50s style rock-and-roll dress and her bright pink hair matched the Japanese blossom tattooed down her arm. She was my best friend and had lined up my next prospective client.

I kissed her cheek. "Hey beautiful."

She beamed a pale pink lip gloss smile up at me, and I sat down at the table. We ordered our usual drinks, and as we waited for them to arrive, I prompted the conversation. "So, tell me about this guy."

"Well," she started, "I met his sister at a job just this last weekend."

"The wedding?" I asked. "How'd it go?" Lola ran her own makeup styling business and weddings were just one of her specialties.

Our drinks arrived. Lola sipped her coffee and I let my tea brew a little longer. "Oh, it went just fine," she said, putting her cup back down on the table. "Anyway, the sister was a bridesmaid, and we got to talking. Her brother's just broken up with his fiancé, and she mentioned that he was trying to get him back."

I smiled.

"So I told her I know a guy," Lola said, looking pointedly at me, "who just might be able to help him with that."

"He's gay?" I asked. She said *he* was trying to get *him* back, but I wanted to be sure.

"Sure is."

I sighed, a little relieved. I had no problem working with straight clients, but batting for my own team was my preferred choice. Especially when public displays of affection were required, sidling up to a stubbled jaw was more my thing than a sweetly perfumed, soft-skinned one.

"What else do you know about him?"

"Just that his sister said he was devastated and probably wouldn't want anything to do with this, but that they'd be here at three." I looked at my watch. It was right on three. Lola patted my hand on the table. "Oh, here they are now."

I looked up at who was walking in. The woman was first, with blondish shoulder length hair, pale skin and a wide smile. She was a beautiful woman. The guy behind her had short sandy-blond hair, and palish skin. He was cute too, in a *normal guy* kind of way. He also looked like he'd rather be anywhere else but here.

Lola and I both stood up, and Lola waved them over. "Sarah, so nice to see you again!"

"You too!" Sarah said. She looked right at me and grinned. "I'm Sarah, and this is my brother, Andrew Landon." She turned to her brother, which of course made both Lola and I look at her brother, and there was Andrew staring at me.

I was used to this.

I didn't exactly fit the "well-adjusted into society" mould. I had a white button-down shirt on with the sleeves rolled up to my elbows, which meant he could see my arms. My full-sleeved tattooed arms. I wore three-quarter brown dress pants and suspenders, loafers, and my hair was shaved at the sides and kinda long on top, and I had a bit of a beard happening. Lola had called my look "lumbersexual hipster" once, and it wasn't until I got home and googled it that I agreed with her. Though I kept my beard short, but it was a beard nonetheless.

"Um, I think this was a mistake," Andrew mumbled and he turned to leave.

Sarah grabbed his arm before he could walk away. "You said you'd hear them out." Andrew stopped and took a deep breath, and although it was clearly not where he wanted to be, he stayed.

I smiled at him. "Take a seat. Let me get you a drink. Coffee?"

Sarah sat down with a tentative, apologetic smile, and waited for her brother to do the same. Andrew sat with a barely contained sigh and forced a somewhat appeased look onto his face. "So, I'm the loser who needs help getting my fiancé back."

I looked at him for a long moment. "No, you have a loser of an ex, who needs reminding of what he's missing."

This must have caught him by surprise. He tilted his head, opened his mouth to say something but promptly snapped it shut. Sarah spoke instead. "We'll just give you boys a minute, okay?" She eyeballed her brother in a be-nice-or-else kinda way, before giving Lola a nod toward the service counter.

When it was just me and Andrew, I leaned back in my chair, smiled and said nothing. I wanted to see how long it would take him to talk. He crossed his arms, then uncrossed them, then shook his head. It wasn't even fifteen seconds. "Look, I don't know how these things work."

"It's easy," I told him. "You tell me everything you know about your ex. Where he works, where he hangs out, where he shops. We just happen to be there, bein' all close and what-not, and make sure he sees us."

"And?"

"And you find out if he wants you back or not."

Andrew frowned at the window that fronted the street and folded his arms. He was silent for nine seconds before he added, "He'll never believe I'm with a guy like you."

"Like me?" I questioned.

"Yes, you're... cool and... hip. And I'm... not."

"I can be anyone you need me to be," I said.

"Do you really pretend to be someone's boyfriend for a living?"

"Yes I do."

"Your accent, are you Australian?"

"Yes I am."

"How did you start out doing this?" he asked. "I mean, it's not exactly a job I'd imagine is advertised."

I nodded toward Lola. "I'd been here in LA for all of a week when I met Lola. She'd just broken up with her guy, and I took her out for coffee. He saw us, thought I was her new boyfriend. He turned into a sappy puddle of goo on the footpath, and my work was done. She joked that it worked so well, I should do it for a living," I told him.

Andrew's brow furrowed. "With her? You worked with women?"

I smiled at him. "I work for whoever pays. But yes, I started out as the 'straight' boyfriend. But then same-sex marriages were a thing, and as a gay man, it was a natural progression for me."

"Are you really gay? Or is it part of the act?"

Fair question, which I had no problems in answering. I leaned in so not everyone in the café could hear. "I'm gay. I like men. I like the feel of stubble. I like hard muscles, not soft feminine skin. I love dick. I like sucking it and being fucked by it, but most of all, I love arse. So yes, I'm gay. Queer as a three-dollar bill."

His mouth fell open and he blinked a few times, shocked at my bluntness. If we were going to do this, he'd get used to it. "I um, I uh..."

"What's your ex's name?"

"Um. Eli."

"How long were you together?"

"Eight months."

"How long ago did he leave?"

His voice was so quiet I barely heard him. "A month ago."

I gave him a moment. He was obviously still hurting. "Are you out? I mean at work, friends, family? Do they know you're gay?"

His eyebrows knitted together and a hint of offence sparked in his eyes. "Yes."

"I only ask because if we do this, I'll have to get to know you pretty well, and there'll be some times where we need to be close in public. Like I might hold your hand, lean in close and talk into your ear, that kind of thing, so Eli can see us being all friendly. For this to work, you need to be comfortable with that. You also need to reciprocate it, so it looks authentic. Can you do that?"

Andrew swallowed hard and shrugged one shoulder. "Um..."

"Andrew, do you want to do this?" I asked him outright. He looked up at the ceiling and puffed out his cheeks as he exhaled, but didn't answer. So I rephrased my question. "Do you want to get Eli back?"

Andrew's gaze darted to mine, and he seemed embarrassed to answer. "Yeah."

I held out my hand for him to shake, which he looked at for a second before he took my hand in his. His strong grip surprised me. "Then let's do this," I said with a grin. I let go of his hand and sat back in my seat. "Okay, first things first. Tell me everything I need to know about you."

Andrew glanced at his sister. "I um, do we have to do this here?" Obviously he didn't really want to go into details in front of his sister in the middle of a café on a busy Friday afternoon. I didn't exactly blame him. Just when I thought this whole agreement might be like pulling teeth, and therefore a mistake, he suggested I meet him at his place the next day.

"Perfect," I agreed. "I'll bring lunch. What's your favourite?"

"My favourite what?"

I almost laughed. "Your favourite thing to have for lunch."

"Oh." He blinked in surprise. He paused, then shook his head. "I'm not fussy."

"You were going to say something but stopped," I said. "Tell me."

He hesitated. "Well, there's a deli not far from where I

live. They make these—" He put his hands out to show me the size of a basketball. "—antipasto salads."

"Okay then," I said with a smile. "Antipasto salads it is. I'll pick some up on my way."

"I can call them ahead of time if you want," he said, then cleared his throat. "If that's okay. I can text you the address."

"Perfect. Make it for twelve thirty."

Andrew nodded and gave me a half smile, and this job was officially moving forward. Figuring it was as good a time as any, we talked about the contract agreement, and I told him my payment terms and conditions—half up front, half at the conclusion, and whilst I guaranteed an outcome, I could never guarantee it would be the outcome he wanted. We exchanged addresses, emails, and phone numbers, shook hands again, and I promised to see him tomorrow.

Lola watched them leave, then took her seat next to me again and nudged me with her elbow. "He's cute."

"He's heartbroken," I amended.

She sighed dramatically. "His sister's really nice."

"Did she say anything?" I asked. "About Andrew or his ex."

Lola shook her head. "Not really. She talked about the wedding last weekend, mostly. It's pretty obvious that she loves her brother though. Everything else you're gonna have to find out on your own." She waggled her eyebrows at me.

I laughed at her. "Starting tomorrow, that's exactly what I plan on doing."

TWO

WITH A BASKETBALL-SIZED SALAD IN HAND, I knocked on Andrew's apartment door. It was a large ground floor apartment in Echo Park, with a cottage feel, complete with white window shutters and decorative handrail. Whether he rented or owned, it was apparent Andrew had some money. Then again, the guys who could afford to pay me usually did.

Andrew opened the door. He wore dark blue jeans and a white button-down shirt. His blond spikey hair was brushed to the side, he was clean shaven, and everything about him said tidy. His smile was a little forced, but he stepped aside and said, "Come in."

I stepped inside—not unaware of how good he smelled— not sure where to go, but headed into the front living room. It was furnished like a proper house, like he had his shit together. A baby grand piano sat in the corner, all shiny and dustless. Matching sofas, different coloured cushions, and framed hand-drawn ink pictures on the walls that tied all the colours together. The room was filled with natural light. Everything was in its place.

I wondered briefly if he'd hired a designer, but looking back at Andrew, and how perfectly put together he was, I had no doubt he did this on his own. I gave him a smile, and he wiped his hands down his thighs, clearly nervous at having me here.

I held out the brown paper bag. "Lunch."

"Right," he said, walking past me. "Um, this way."

I followed him through a door at the end of the room, which led to a small, well-appointed kitchen. He collected two plates and some cutlery. "May I get you a drink?"

I found myself smiling at him. "Yes, you may. Water would be fine."

He paused, probably not sure if I was taking the piss or not, before he took two bottles of water from his fridge. We sat down at the small table just off the kitchen, in front of a large window that overlooked a courtyard. "Nice place," I said, as we started to eat.

He looked up at the window like he'd forgotten it was there. "Thanks."

"How long have you lived here?"

"Just over twelve months."

He didn't offer any more information willingly. I took another mouthful of the salad. "Mmm, this is good." And it was. A mix of marinated artichoke, eggplant, capsicums, beets, pasta spirals, and rocket leaves.

He nodded and swallowed his food. "It is. They also do a range of homemade pastries and soups which I love in winter, but their salad bar is my favourite."

"So," I prompted him, now that he was talking at least. "Tell me the Andrew Landon story."

His fork stopped half way to his mouth. "There's not a great deal to tell."

I looked at him for a long moment. He clearly had a self-esteem issue. "Well, there's a beautiful piano out there that begs to differ."

He almost smiled. "My parents had me in lessons from the age of four."

"Classical?"

He nodded and ate his forkful of salad. I waited for him to swallow it so he'd continue. "My sister did ballet; I did piano," he offered. "My parents are theatre people."

"And they know you're gay?" It wasn't really a question, because he'd already told me the answer yesterday.

He blinked and delicately put his fork on his empty plate, perfectly centred, twelve to six o'clock, whereas mine was thrown on at about ten to four. "Yes, they know."

"Is it an issue for them?"

He shook his head a little. "No. It's not an issue."

A part of me sighed with relief inside. I always dreaded asking the parental question. "I'm sorry if some of these questions are personal," I told him. "But that's what I'm here for. I need to get to know you."

He nodded. "That's okay. I'm just not used to it, that's all."

"If there's anything you think that crosses a line, just call *veto*, and I'll back off," I said. "We have a goal here, and that's to get Eli to realise he made a mistake. But that doesn't mean open season on your personal life. I will respect your boundaries."

He nodded again and visibly relaxed. He even gave me a smile before he cleared away the plates. "Thank you for lunch."

"My pleasure. I can see why it's your favourite. It was delicious."

He smiled as he put the plates in the sink. "Shall we move to the living room? It's more comfortable."

"We shall."

He paused again, obviously not liking me repeating his words, but still he said nothing.

"I'm not taking the piss," I said, standing up from the table. "In fact, I like the way you speak. It's cool to hear someone actually use the English language as it was intended. It's a nice change."

He frowned again, as though he liked the insult more than the compliment, before walking out to the living room. He sat on the end of the three-seater sofa, so I followed his lead but sat myself right in the middle. I positioned myself kinda side-on to him and folded one leg up under the other, careful not to put my boot on the sofa, and dived right in for the details. "So, tell me about you."

He was back to being nervous, sitting up straight with his hands balled into fists on his thighs. "Well, what do you want to know?"

"How old are you?"

"Twenty six."

"What do you do for work?"

"I'm a visual animator."

What? "No way!"

"Um, yeah. I work for DreamWorks."

"Shut the front door."

Andrew looked to the front door. "Um..."

"Seriously?" I asked with a laugh. "An animator for DreamWorks?"

He nodded and bit his lip. "It's not that exciting. I mean, I love it, but it's fastidious work. It might sound glamorous, but it's a very slow and arduous job."

"I am so impressed," I said, shaking my head. "I cannot believe that's what you do."

He blushed, but his brow furrowed. "Um, why can't you believe it? Do I not seem the type?"

Oh God, he thought I thought he wasn't good enough. "No, I mean if you'd said you were in finance or law, I would've thought okay, cool."

"Do you think I'm boring?"

I snorted. "No. Not boring. I think you're serious. Serious but very interesting. And what's to say people in finance and law are boring anyway. Who knows? Maybe there's some interesting corporate lawyer or finance consultants *somewhere* in the world. They haven't found any yet, but it's not *imp*ossible."

He almost smiled.

"So do you work on films?" I asked, unable to hide my excitement. I knew LA was full of entertainment industry people, but animation and cartoonography? Well, that was something else. "Have I seen your work? Please tell me you worked on Shrek, because that is the funniest movie ever!"

"Uh, no. I don't work on film as such," he said, apologetically. "Anyway, for me to have worked on Shrek, I'd have been ten years old."

"Oh, right."

He seemed amused. "Have you been to Universal Studios?"

"Nope."

He blinked. "Oh, okay then." My answer seemed to throw him. "Well, they have animations throughout. Or the promotional shots, I work on those. Some cover artwork, that kind of thing."

"Wow, that's incredible," I told him. He bit his lip, but it was clear my approval pleased him. "Tell me what you do every day. What's a typical day at work for you?"

He cleared his throat. "Well, I work at the animation studio in Glendale. I start at eight thirty. We have a lot of team meetings, that kind of thing, in the mornings usually.

Um, I'm technically a Look Development Artist. You know the storyboards with hand-drawn characters and scenes on them? That's what I do. For promotional work."

"Wow."

He fought a smile and picked at his thumbnail in his lap. "We're given a directive from HQ. We do the boards with scenes and characters from the movie and then hand it over to the art department. They make it adaptable, then it goes to sets and a few other teams before it gets to animation."

I shook my head. "Uh, I'm so impressed."

"It's not like I'm developing original characters or anything," he said, downplaying himself completely. "It's actually pretty easy to take established characters and landmarks and work with those instead."

"Well, I'm still impressed. It's fascinating." Then I noticed the framed artwork on the wall again. "Oh my God," I said, getting up and walking over to them. There were three square frames, each showcasing an abstract ink-drawn human and his horse with a funny tail...? No, not a horse, a dog? No wait... it was a dragon... *Oh holy shit!* It was from *How to Train Your Dragon*. It wasn't the characters that were coloured, it was the background, but only barely. It was beyond abstract. It was stunning. "You did these?"

Andrew nodded. "My first ever boards. They let me keep them. They weren't the finished product anyway, just sketches, really." He walked over and stood beside me. "I finished them here and added the colours to the background later."

I was still in awe of his talents. "It's like a watercolour," I murmured. I stared at him until he turned to look at me. "Andrew, they are amazing."

He blushed and swallowed hard before giving me a shy smile. "Thank you."

"You should do art."

He blinked in surprise. "I do art."

"No, not for movies or promotional studio stuff," I corrected. "But for art galleries and that kind of art. Seriously."

He shook his head at me and went back to the sofa. "Why? I have the best job in the world."

"True." I sat beside him and gave one last look to the framed boards. "And just so you know, I loved that movie."

Now he laughed. His whole face changed when he smiled with abandon. He got those little wrinkles at the corners of his eyes, and his eyes glittered somehow. His laugh was deep and contagious. "What?" I said indignantly, but smiling. "I happen to like animated movies." But I didn't want him to lose his good mood, so I asked him more questions before he went all quiet on me again. "Tell me about the people you work with."

"They're all good people," he said. "We have a certain freedom at work. I would be— how did you put it?—the serious one, I guess."

"I didn't mean that in a bad way," I added.

"Oh, I know," he offered. "It's true. I've always been that way. The quiet, serious one. For the most part."

"You know what they say about that," I said with a smile. "It's the quiet ones you have to watch."

Andrew scoffed out a laugh. "Well, I don't know about that."

I needed to keep asking him questions. But I'd seen yesterday how he'd clam up and not want to answer anything if he was backed into a corner, so I needed to stay on safer topics.

"Okay, quick fire questions," I said. "Food you can't stand?"

"Avocado. It's slimy and wrong."

"Coffee?"

"Yes."

"How do you like it?"

"Latte with two percent. No sugar or syrups."

"What day do you do your laundry?"

"Saturdays."

Oh. "Am I interrupting your laundry?"

He smirked. "No. I live dangerously like that."

I laughed. "Gym membership?"

"Yes."

"Allergic to dogs?"

"No."

"Cats?"

"No."

"Horses?"

He laughed. "No."

"Favourite movie?"

He glanced up at the wall at the framed drawings and smiled. "*How to Train Your Dragon 2*."

"Unfair!" I cried. "Okay, favourite movie you haven't worked on."

"Um." He smiled again and looked up like the answer was written on the ceiling. "*Blade Runner* or *A Clockwork Orange*."

"Okay, stop," I said, putting my hands up. "You can't just go from cutesy animated DreamWorks to gritty Ridley Scott and Stanley Kubrick."

He was clearly surprised that I was familiar with the directors. "Were there rules?" he countered.

"Well, no."

"Next question."

I let out an incredulous laugh. "I can't just leave that. Seriously? *A Clockwork Orange*?"

"I also love the classics like *Frankenstein* and *The Wizard of Oz*."

I shook my head. "You are a complex man."

He was grinning now. He really was very good looking. "Not really."

"Yes, really. Favourite book?"

"Oh, um." He squinted, as though it pained him to pick just one. "*To Kill a Mocking Bird*. I know, it's everyone's favourite book." He shrugged.

"Well, there's a reason why it's everyone's favourite," I added. "Favourite song?"

He put his hand up. "No. Too many to choose from."

"Everyone has an all-time favourite song."

He shook his head. "Do you?"

"Yes."

"What is it?"

"Not telling. Today is all for questions about you, not me."

"When is it your turn to answer questions?"

"Tomorrow."

"We're meeting tomorrow?"

"Yep."

"Where at?"

"My place," I offered without any clue as to why. The words were out before I could stop them. "If you want. Or we can go someplace else, I don't mind."

"And you'll tell me what your favourite song is then?"

"Yep, as long as you narrow yours down to one. One favourite song."

He smiled and shook his head. "I could call veto."

I grinned back at him. "You could, but you won't. Okay, so tell me about your friends."

He paused. "Will you want to meet them?" he asked, his smile was gone and there was caution in his eyes.

"That depends," I answered with a shrug, trying to be casual. It was like I'd hit a nerve. "If I need to, I guess I will. But right now I just need to know what makes you tick." Then I asked, "Would you have a problem with me meeting them?"

He was quick to answer. "Oh, no, no. It'd be fine, I guess." He shook his head. "I just didn't know how far this went, that's all. I don't want them to get the wrong idea about us, and I'd prefer not to tell anyone that this"—he motioned between us—"is a contract deal."

"It goes as far as we need it to go, and you can tell people whatever you're comfortable in telling them," I told him with what I hoped was a reassuring smile. "It goes as far as getting Eli to see us together and hopefully make him see what he walked away from. And that's all."

Andrew nodded and looked back down at his hands.

I took a deep breath. "Okay, so tell me about him."

"What do you want to know?"

"Full name."

"Eli Masterson."

"How old is he?"

"Twenty five."

"Where did you meet?"

He smiled. "In the grocery store."

"Who asked who out?"

Andrew blinked, and he answered softly. "He asked me."

"Do you have any pictures of him?"

Andrew fished his phone out of his pocket. He thumbed through some pages, then handed it to me. "There's a few," he said. "You can scroll through if you like."

Eli had dark hair, dark eyes, olive skin, and a toothy

smile. The first picture was of them taking a selfie. Eli was holding something in his hands. Andrew was holding the phone so I assumed the photo was his idea. I scrolled back to another one and it was a candid of Eli, then another of him poking his tongue out. Then one of them sitting together, the photo taken by someone else. They looked happy enough though, and it really wasn't like I knew Andrew very well—and I'd never even laid eyes on Eli. They looked decidedly normal.

"How long were you together?"

"Eight months," Andrew said.

"And you lived together?"

He nodded. "We'd only been dating for a month or two when he moved in." He laughed, an incredulous sound. "That sounds so stupid, I know. But he was here almost every day anyway, and he was paying rent for an apartment he was never at, so it made sense." Andrew sighed long and loud. "Our whole relationship was a bit of a whirlwind. Everything happened so quickly."

"You were engaged?"

"Yes." Then he shrugged one shoulder. "Well, not techni-cally. We didn't have rings or anything. He asked me to marry him, but then he never brought it up again."

Hmm. Strange.

There was something I had to know. "Andrew, can I ask you something personal?"

He laughed. "And you haven't already?"

I smiled at that. True as it was, this was different. "Did he hurt you?"

Andrew froze, then blinked. "When he left me?"

"No, I mean, did he ever hurt you? Was he rough, intimi-dating, or aggressive in any way?"

"What? No," he shot back. "No, nothing like that at all. He

was never like that. Why would you ask that? Do you think I'd want him back if he did?"

I put my hand up in a peace-offering kind of way. "I just needed to know what I was dealing with and whether some jealous psycho would want me dead for being with you. I ask everyone that." Well, technically I didn't; I only asked that question if it was warranted.

He took his phone back like I'd offended Eli's photograph. "He's not like that at all. I know some people didn't like him much, but they didn't know him like I did."

"Fair enough," I said. "I meant no harm." He said Eli never hurt him physically, and I believed him. There was just something about Eli that didn't sit well with me. Maybe once I got to know him better, I'd change my mind. Andrew clearly loved him, and my objective was to get them back together, not to see if Eli was worth his salt. "When did you speak to him last?"

"Last week," Andrew said, talking to the photo of Eli.

"Who initiated contact?"

Andrew cleared his throat. "I called him."

"And how was it?" I asked. "Was he amicable about it? Friendly?"

He nodded. "Yes. Chatted and laughed like nothing had changed."

Mixed signals were the worst to deal with. They kept 'em tagging along like a second-hand toy. Discarded in case something better came along, but keeping them close in case it didn't.

He was still staring at his hands in his lap. "Do you think I'm being stupid?"

"Not at all," I replied without hesitation. "You're in love with him. You do whatever it takes. I'm certainly not one to judge."

His eyes shot to mine, his voice whisper quiet. "Have you ever? You know, been in love?"

And just like that, with a surprise question, I got that tight-chested feeling, like his words squeezed my heart. I was going to lie, but then thought fuck it. There was something about Andrew that made me feel, well, I wasn't sure. Safe? Like he wouldn't judge me. So, with that in mind, I told him the truth. "I don't think so. Lust, sure. But love?" I shook my head. "I think love's for other people."

Andrew studied me for a minute, like I confused him. "Do you have someone... a boyfriend?"

I shook my head. "Nope. No time really. I'm too busy going on pretend dates with hot guys like you."

Andrew scoffed and a slight blush crept up his neck. He was apparently at a loss for words. "You say the most random things."

It was true. I did. I needed to know him and Eli, and of course, how and why their relationship ended. So I asked him one more. It was always the hardest question. "Why did he leave you?"

He looked at me like I'd slapped him. He didn't answer for a while. His lips pulled into a twisted pout before his teeth worried over his bottom lip again. Finally he said, "To be honest, I don't know. Like I said, everything was a whirlwind with him. We met, he moved in, he asked me to marry him, everything was going well. Well, I thought it was, then..." He shrugged. "Then I came home from work as he was walking out with his suitcase."

"What did he say?" I asked gently.

"Just that he—" Andrew exhaled loudly. "—just that he needed space."

"So he didn't say it was over? He didn't say the engagement was off?"

Andrew looked at me sadly and shook his head. "No. He said he needed space and just left, like he was heading out to get some milk or something."

"Hmm." Something was off for sure. I frowned, a look Andrew didn't miss.

"What?"

Then for the second hardest question. "Do you think there could be someone else?"

"No." Andrew shook his head, then his brow furrowed. "Well, I don't think so." Then he looked at me with panic in his eyes. "Oh, God. What if there is?" He looked ill before he put his head in his hands.

I put my arm around his shoulder, and went for a well-rehearsed line, only this time it felt different. "Andrew, listen to me. If this guy is seeing someone else, then you're better off without him. But if he just needed space and some time to see things clearly, then we'll put things into focus for him, okay?"

Andrew took a deep breath and composed himself. Finally, he nodded. "Okay."

"Okay then," I said with a reassuring smile. "So if we're gonna get this man of yours all jealous and grovelling at your feet, begging for you to take him back, then we've got work to do."

THREE

"I'm telling you, it was incredible," I said. Lola, Gabriel, Daniela, and Emilio all stared at me. We were having coffee in the tattoo shop, sitting where the clients waited their turn, or went through ink magazines, which had become a Sunday morning brunch tradition with us. Well, I was having my usual green tea, they were having coffee, and I was getting the typical interrogation after I started a new job. *What's he like? Is he a creeper? Does he have a rubber doll fetish?* You know, the usual.

"He has artwork on his living room wall that he did himself," I told them. "It was done with pencil but then the background was watercolour ink. It was freakin' art." I nodded toward the tattoo books on the coffee table between us. "Better than anything I've seen in those."

"Yeah?" Emilio asked. I knew as a tattoo artist he'd appreciate what I was saying. "But he draws cartoons?"

"He does those visual boards that go to the animators," I explained. "It's really very cool. And he has a grand piano in his living room."

"So, no life-like, synthetic sex dolls hiding in his closet?" Daniela asked. She sounded disappointed.

Emilio scowled playfully at her. "Not everyone's a pervert like you."

She grinned at her husband. "Thanks, babe." It made me laugh. Emilio and Daniela had become very close friends of mine. Landlords yes, but Emilio had become like a big brother to me, and his beautiful wife a sister by association.

"So, he's cute *and* completely normal?" Lola asked.

I shrugged. "I don't know him that well, like I haven't seen his sex-toy drawer yet, but yeah. If there's any such thing as normal. And I'm tellin' ya, it's a nice change from the last guy."

Gabriel snorted out a laugh. "Oh come on," he said. "What's wrong with a twenty-something-year-old guy having spoon collections and plastic covered sofas?"

I shook my head, remembering when I first walked into that guy's place. It made me shudder. "That was the least of that guy's problems. He was creepy as hell."

Lola laughed. "Or the asshole super-rich guy before him. Who thought his boyfriend was a commodity to be acquired and couldn't understand why the poor guy ran for the hills."

"I told that guy to run for the hills," I said. "I preferred the guy who covered everything in plastic and Clorox over that arsehole." I could cope with the creepiness of Raymond, but Gerard the self-entitled, self-made millionaire thought his money could buy him whatever he wanted, including people. And that shit didn't fly with me.

"So when's Piano Man getting here?" Emilio asked.

We always had nicknames for my clients. *Clorox Man, Arsehole Super Rich Guy, Dog Hair Guy, Butt Man.* There were made up names for all of them. But for some reason, I didn't like the idea of labelling Andrew with a name that made him less than he was.

"His name is Andrew," I told them. I ignored the looks they gave me and the way Daniela's mouth fell open. "And he'll be here any minute."

Right on cue, Andrew, looking all nerdy-proper-handsome in his argyle sweater and dress pants, stopped out front of the store. He looked up at the name of the shop, completely oblivious to the five people watching him from inside. He shook his head a little, mumbled something to himself, and put his hand up to knock, second guessed himself, then put it down. He took a deep breath and quickly rapped on the door, probably before he lost his nerve and walked away.

"Go save him," Lola said, nudging me with her high-heeled foot.

I realised then I was sitting there like an idiot just watching him. "Right," I said, quickly heading for the door. I unbolted it and swung it inwards. "Hey," I said in greeting.

Andrew gave me a half-smile. "Hi."

I stood aside. "Come in, meet my crew." Andrew stepped inside, smelling all sorts of good, and I locked the door behind him because technically the shop didn't open for another hour or so. He stood there, looking lost and out of place, staring at everyone staring back at him. He looked like he either wanted to pass out or leave. Probably both. "Andrew," I started, putting my hand on his shoulder and urging him forward a little. "This is Daniela and her husband Emilio, they own the shop. And you've met Lola already, but this is her boyfriend Gabriel, or Gabe, as we call him. Guys, this is Andrew."

The four of them waved, said quiet hellos, and made awkward small talk. Andrew wiped his palms on his thighs, so before any of them could say anything to make him feel any more uncomfortable than he already was, and still with my hand on his back, I looked at Andrew and said, "You ready?"

He nodded quickly. "Sure."

Turning to my friends, who were watching us and smiling, I said, "We'll be off. Catch ya's later. Wanna lock the door behind us?" I went to the front door, unlocked it, and held it open for Andrew.

Just before the door closed behind me, I swear I heard Lola do that whisper-squeal thing she does when she's excited. "Oh my God! Did you see Spencer's face?" There was mumbling from the others and someone laughed, but thankfully the door clicked shut before I could hear any more. By some grace of God or good manners, Andrew didn't seem to notice, either. I made a mental note to kill my so-called friends later.

I pointed up the street toward the beach. "This way."

After half a block of silence and small talk about his drive to my place, he said, "Your friends seem nice."

I laughed. "They don't normally behave like that. They're really good people. Most people think tattoo artists are thugs, but that's not the case. Emilio and Daniela are very loyal friends to me, and Lola... well, she's crazy. But she's my best friend. Sweet, fierce, and crazy."

"Not many people could pull off having pink hair, a black and white striped dress, and teal pumps," he said.

I was grinning now. "No, they couldn't. She pretty much nails that 50s pin-up girl meets punk rocker look."

He smiled. "She does."

"There's a little Moroccan tea house around the corner," I told him, nodding up the street. "They do a great breakfast. Have you eaten?"

"A few hours ago."

God, it was ten o'clock on a Sunday. "You've been up for hours already?"

"Been to the gym too."

I shook my head at him. "Then you've worked up an appetite."

"I've never had Moroccan before. Certainly not for breakfast."

I held the door to the café open and found myself smiling at him. "Then today will be your first."

Inside the café was a mix of oranges, purples, and reds. It smelled of spice and lemon. The dark wooden tables were low and the bench seats covered with cushions, and I was thankful my favourite table was still empty. It was in the corner by the window where the sunlight filtered in.

I took a seat and waited for Andrew to do the same. He sat across from me, looking around, smiling. "I love this place," I told him. "And this table? If I could bring a book and have them serve me tea all day, I'd never leave. Especially in winter when the sun comes through the window."

He smiled, the eye-crinkling kind of smile, and I was, again, struck by how good looking he was. His sandy-blond hair was cut short and brushed to the side but still a bit spikey. He was clean-shaven and smelled really freakin' good: like soap, deodorant, and man. He had that clean-cut all-American-guy thing down pat. I tried to imagine him wearing something more my style or anything different than the argyle sweater and dress pants, for that matter, but couldn't. It suited him so perfectly. If there was a magazine called *Sexy Nerds*, he'd be on the cover.

The owner, an older, motherly woman by the name of Zineb, came over and gave me a smile. "Spencer, not seen you in a while."

"I know! I've been busy this week," I told her. "But my

friend here has never had Moroccan. What do you think he should try?"

"*Khobz b'chehma* with lamb and peppers," she said. "Made fresh this morning, and *msemen* because it's your favourite."

I grinned at her. "As always. With your fig and honey jam, please."

She rolled her eyes. "Of course. Tea?"

"For me, yes please." I waved my hand at Andrew, who was watching on amused. "And a latte, with two percent, no sugar or syrups. Thank you." I requested his order exactly how he told me he liked it.

Zineb left us and started hollering Arabic at her husband. God, I loved this place.

"You remembered?" Andrew said. "How I take my coffee."

"Sure," I replied. Jeez, it was like no one had ever done such a simple thing for him. "It's my job to remember everything about you."

"Yeah, of course," he said, suddenly finding the menu interesting.

"And that reminds me," I added. "I need that favourite song."

"Well, you see, it's not quite that simple."

"Yes it is."

"Then what's your one favourite song, above all others?"

"Jeff Buckley's cover of 'Hallelujah.'"

He blinked. "Just like that?"

"Just like that."

"It's a good song."

"It's the perfect song," I amended. "I like Leonard Cohen's version, don't get me wrong. But Jeff Buckley's version is, well, it's perfect."

"Perfect? That's a pretty big call." He frowned. "The perfect song? How do you define the perfect song?"

I found myself smiling at him. "Don't overthink it, that's how. Discard all the technical crap, the parameters, the chords, whatever. Go by feel. How it feels in here." I pressed my hand against my breastbone. "That song will stop me wherever I am."

He was staring at me with a hint of a smile on his lips, but there was an understanding, an unspoken agreement in his eyes. "Well, if that's how you determine the perfect song, then I'd have to say Beethoven's *Moonlight Sonata*." He swallowed hard then shrugged, like he was sorry. "It's not cool or anything like that, but it's a beautiful song. Well, technically it's not even a song. It's a musical composition."

"Technicalities aside, don't apologise," I said. "Ever. If you love it, then own it. Repeat after me..." He stared, waiting. So I said, "My favourite song is the musical composition Beethoven's *Moonlight Sonata*, because it's fucking awesome."

He laughed and looked around to see who might have heard me swear.

"Say it," I urged him.

He cleared his throat, and spoke softly. "My favourite song is Beethoven's *Moonlight Sonata*, because it's... fucking awesome."

I grinned at him. "See? Isn't that much better?"

He chuckled, just as Zineb bought us our drinks. She looked at me, expectantly. "So?" she said. "Who is your friend?"

Andrew stared up at her and froze, and I made introductions. "This is Andrew. Andrew this is Zineb, maker of the finest green tea in LA."

She beamed. "He like Moroccan green tea," she said to Andrew. "Not many people do. Buy him this, you'll win his heart." I snorted, and Andrew almost swallowed his tongue.

"Food won't be long," she added before walking off, seemingly oblivious to the look of horror on Andrew's face.

"She thinks we're...?"

I nodded. "Better get used to it," I said, turning my cup of tea. "We need the public to think we are dating. Especially Eli."

Andrew's brow knitted together, but he nodded. "Yeah. I guess."

"I'm not that scary, am I?" I asked, half joking, half not.

"What? No!" he said vehemently. "You're just, you know."

"Uh, no. I don't know." This could end badly. I almost didn't want to ask. "Is that a good *you know* or a bad *you know*?"

"Good," he said quickly. A faint blush crept up his neck. "It's just that you're all... trendy." He cringed at the word. "And I'm not."

"Well, excuse me Mr *A Clockwork Orange* and *Moonlight Sonata* lover," I said with a smile. "That's pretty damn cool."

He shook his head, dismissing me entirely. "But look at how you dress."

I looked at what I was wearing. My three-quarter tan dress pants, white button-down shirt, and blue-suede Oxfords. "Is there something wrong with the way I dress?" I asked. I'd never had anyone not like the way I dressed. "I was going to wear my suspenders but didn't."

He shook his head. "There's nothing wrong with it. And I happen to like suspenders on you. You look like you're straight out of the pages of *Trendy LA*."

I snorted. "You do the magazine thing too?" I asked. "I had you from *Sexy Nerd*," I admitted. He let out a disbelieving laugh. "But I had *you* on the cover. Not just some page four random like you had me. Oh no, I had you on the cover, my friend."

He laughed quietly and sipped his coffee. "Okay, I'll concede you a cover shot."

I grinned at him. "Thanks!"

"*Sexy Nerd*," he repeated softly, shaking his head. "You're delusional."

"I do believe you fit both categories," I said, turning my cup of tea. "And fit them well, I might add. I like how you dress."

He blushed again, even the tips of his ears turned pink.

I stuck my foot out. "Anyway, I love these shoes. I paid a fortune for them."

"I can tell," he said, admiring my loafers.

I held out my arms, where ink covered every part of my skin from my rolled-up shirtsleeve to my wrists. "Do you not like my tattoos?"

He froze again, but before he could answer, Zineb brought our food over. "You boys share?" she asked.

"Yes please," I said, making room on the table. "We'll have a bit of both." Zineb put the food down, sorted out plates and cutlery, and left us to it. "Try the savoury first," I told him. "It's so good. It's spiced lamb and Mediterranean vegetables done in a flatbread. And the msemen are like pancakes. Zineb's husband makes this fig and honey jam. It's divine."

He took a forkful of the khobz b'chehma and moaned. It was a throaty sound that made my skin tingle. He swallowed it down. "Okay, wow."

I laughed, trying to ignore my reaction to him. "It's good, yes?"

He nodded and continued to eat. In between mouthfuls, he asked, "So, my turn to ask questions?"

Shit. I nodded. "Yep."

"What part of Australia are you from?"

"Sydney."

"And you've been here two years?"

I nodded, washing food down with a sip of tea. "Yep."

"Why did you leave?"

I considered how to best answer. I didn't need to go dredging up family history for a guy who, in all likelihood I'd know for a month then never see again, so I decided on answering diplomatically. "I hated my job and wanted to travel. Airfares to LA were on sale, so I packed a bag and here I am."

He seemed to process that for a while. Whether he believed me or not, I had no clue. But it seemed he did. "Family?"

Jesus. Okay, so maybe he didn't. I needed to work on my ability to lie. "Parents, still married. Two brothers. Both younger than me."

"They didn't mind you moving to the other side of the world?"

"Nope."

"Have they visited you here?" he pressed. "Or have you been back since?"

I had a mouthful of food, so it wasn't like I could have spoken, even if I wanted to. I couldn't tell the truth on this one. I shook my head.

"Do you miss them?"

"Yes." It came out a little quicker than I'd meant.

He nodded, more to himself than to me, and I knew right then he saw straight through me. Thankfully, he didn't push, and he changed the subject. "Favourite food?"

"You're eating it."

"Least favourite?"

"Shellfish. I'm allergic."

His fork stopped halfway to his mouth. "Seriously?"

I pulled an EpiPen from my pocket and held it up for him

to see. "Very. I usually carry one of these with me if I'm eating out somewhere new, and as a general rule I don't eat anything that comes out of the water." Then as a joke, I added, "Unless he showers first."

Andrew laughed at that. "So no seafood."

I shook my head and pocketed the EpiPen. "Nope. To be safe, I don't eat anything that comes out of the water, like fish, even though it's technically not shellfish. I also don't eat many Asian foods because they use fish sauce as a base for a lot of meals. I have to ask a lot of restaurants before I can eat there, but some don't get it. Like Thai beef salad? You'd think it was okay because it's beef and salad, but it has fish sauce in the dressing. But even the guys I work with, like faux-dating" —I motioned between us—"I have to ask them not to eat anything that might be contaminated as well. Because if we need to make out and he's just eaten lobster, me going into anaphylactic shock in front of his ex doesn't look good."

He looked shocked. "Has that ever happened?"

I gave him a smile. "No."

He made a thoughtful face, and he put his fork on his empty plate. "Do you have to make out with all your clients?"

"Are you asking if we have to kiss?"

He nodded.

"If it will get Eli's attention, then yes. If it will make him want to throw you over his shoulder and take you back to his cave to make you his again, then yes." I let him think about that for a moment, no doubt that visual was playing over in his mind. "I promise, I have excellent dental hygiene, extra soft lips, and only give tongue if it's warranted."

He did that barked-out laugh again and blushed. *God, he was too easy.* "Oh, um, right."

I swapped the plates over and served up the pancakes and put the jam on the side for him to taste. It also gave him some time to compose himself. "So I was thinking, this afternoon we could go over Eli's schedules, if that's okay with you?"

"Oh." He swallowed hard. "Sure. I guess."

"We can do some sleuthing," I explained. "Stalk his Facebook, see where he's been, that kind of thing."

He nodded thoughtfully. "Okay."

"Do you know where he's been living?"

He frowned, then shook his head. "No."

"Where does he work?"

"Downtown."

"What does he do?"

"He works at a printing press on Wilshire."

That wasn't too far. "Hobbies? Gym? Favourite bars?"

"He has a membership at the same gym as me, but I haven't seen him there since," Andrew said. "We went to a few of the bars in Echo Park, though they weren't really my scene."

"What's your scene?"

He cleared his throat. "There's a jazz bar not far from his work. The food's great, the music is incredible."

"You like jazz?"

He nodded. "Love it." Then he innocently took a mouthful of the Moroccan pancakes with fig and honey jam, and he moaned. A deep, throaty, delicious sound that sent shivers over my skin and a pleasant ache straight to my dick. "Oh, my God," he murmured.

I was staring at him. That sound, Jesus. If he moaned like that over food, I'd love to hear him in bed.

"What?" he said, snapping me out of my lust-daze.

Shit. I got caught gawking. I shifted in my seat, trying to quell the desire that was filling my cock, and cleared my throat. "The pancakes are good, yes?"

He nodded. "So good." He took another mouthful, and

this time he sighed instead of moaned. I was almost disappointed.

Zineb appeared at the table with a knowing smile. "He like the conserve, yes?" she asked and nudged me with her elbow. "Unless he make that sound for you. You like it, Spencer, I can tell."

Andrew almost dropped his fork, but it was me who was embarrassed. I felt a heat rush over my cheeks and I laughed to hide it, but I was blushing. Jesus Christ. I wanted to die.

Andrew's shock turned to embarrassment, though he didn't go as red as me, I'm sure of it. "Was I loud?"

I scoffed. "Uh, yeah."

"Oh," he said softly. He wasn't laughing. He looked up at Zineb. "I apologise."

She just picked up the empty plate from the table and laughed it off. "No being sorry. Spencer here liked it." She patted my shoulder and walked back to the counter, and a whole new level of embarrassment washed over me.

"I'm really embarrassed," he whispered.

Shit. I reached over and grabbed his hand and gave it a squeeze. I didn't let it go. "Don't be. It's my fault. I shouldn't have..." I shook my head. "Wanna get out of here?"

He nodded. So still holding his hand, I stood up and walked over to the counter. I only dropped his hand so I could pay the bill. I gave Zineb my card, praying like hell she wouldn't embarrass me further.

No such luck. She smiled sweetly at me. "It makes me so happy to see Spencer finally with a man who make him smile."

I considered praying to the earthquake gods to give the San Andreas a nudge so the ground would split open and swallow me whole. Instead I stood there like an idiot, turned a darker shade of pink, and mumbled, "Thank you, Zineb, for not embarrassing me at all today."

She handed me back my bankcard, looking confused. "What? You not love this boy?"

I shook my head and swallowed the lump in my throat, which could have possibly been my heart. "Thanks, Zineb. We'll see you next time, 'kay?"

She looked even more confused. "But Spencer you don't look at the other boys like you look at this one."

Needing to not be in the firing line of Zineb's embarrassing untruths for one second longer, I grabbed Andrew's hand and all but dragged him out of the café, waving Zineb off as I went. As soon as I was a good twenty meters up the street, I dropped his hand so I could put both hands on my knees and catch my breath.

Andrew surprised me by laughing. I would have expected a list of reactions from anger to embarrassment, even outrage. But laughing? I looked up at him. "What's so funny?"

"You," he answered. "The look on your face."

"She embarrassed the hell outta me!"

"She embarrassed you? She made a point of telling the whole café I make noises that you like!"

"Well, your sex sounds are fucking hot, I have to say."

His eyes popped and his mouth fell open. "My what?"

Now it was my turn to laugh. I stood up straight. "Never mind. Let's just agree to forget everything she said."

He stared at me. "My sex sounds?"

"The way you moaned," I explained, needing to clear my throat. "It was um, sexy as hell."

He folded his arms, then unfolded them, then shoved his hands into his pockets. He looked rather pissed off, but the burning blush that crept up his neck gave him away. "Well. Do you make a habit of saying inappropriate things?"

"Only when guys make inappropriate noises that make me think dirty thoughts, which leads me to saying such things out loud." I shrugged. "And anyway, it wasn't inappropriate of me to speak the truth. The noise you made was hot."

He covered his eyes with his hand. "Oh God." Then his hand fell away and he stared at me. "I can't believe you just said that."

"I can't believe you don't already know that," I replied. "Has no one ever told you?"

He looked kind of horrified. "We're not having this conversation. I call veto."

I laughed and nodded back toward the tattoo shop. "Come on, we've got super-sleuthing to do on this fella of yours."

The shop was open, so I held the door for Andrew. "After you."

He stepped inside and shoved his hands in his pockets, a sure sign he was nervous, or unsure. Emilio was at his work station and a familiar face was in the chair with his chest exposed having his skin inked. "Hey Spencer!" Eric said, extending his arm.

I bumped my fist to his. "Hey man." Eric was a regular here. I had a closer look at his ever-growing chest piece. "Lookin' good."

Emilio didn't look up from his work when he said, "Hey Spence, can you grab me some alcohol swabs?"

"Sure thing," I said, going straight to the cabinet he kept them in. I put the box on his trolley beside his arm. "Lola and Gabe still here?"

"Yep," came Lola's reply. "Stall two."

I nodded to Andrew, a silent invitation for him to follow me, and led him to the back of the shop to the private cubicles. The curtain was slightly open so I stuck my head in. Gabe was lying on the table and Lola and Daniela were standing over him, inspecting his clamped nipple. "Hey," I said with a laugh. "Do I even wanna know?"

Gabe rolled his eyes. "Lola wants to pierce my nipples."

I walked in, and Andrew stood at the door with a look on his face that was a mix of shock and morbid curiosity. I peeked over Lola's shoulder at Gabe's stretched and clamped nipple. It wasn't pierced yet, but Lola was holding the piercing needle.

"You're gonna do it?" I asked.

She nodded excitedly. "Daniela is supervising, but yeah, I get to pierce his skin and leave this pretty little barbell in its place." Daniela was the resident body piercer and would have made sure everything was perfect.

Gabe sighed. "I'm starting to think my girlfriend has a pain kink."

I snorted. "Only if it's your pain, my friend."

"Do you want yours done?" Daniela asked.

I instinctively put my hands over my nipples. "No."

"It's more pleasure than pain," Daniela said, waggling her eyebrows. "Believe me."

"What about a Prince Albert?" Lola asked.

My dick retracted into my body. "Jesus, no."

After she stopped laughing, Lola looked at Andrew. "How was breakfast?"

Andrew smiled at her. "Good. We had Moroccan. Apparently I made sex sounds, and Zineb said Spencer's in love with me."

Everyone stared at him for a full three seconds of stunned silence before I burst out laughing. I couldn't believe he just said that. "You weren't supposed to tell them that!"

Andrew chuckled and looked at my friends. "You should have seen him blush."

I looked straight at Lola. "He's lying. He has compulsive lying disorder and makes shit up all the time."

Andrew laughed, but when Lola, Daniela, and Gabe all turned to look at him, he just slowly shook his head. "It was the truth."

"Okay," I said, clapping my hands together. "On that note, we'll just be going."

I tried to usher Andrew out the door, but he looked around me to Gabe's stretched nipple and frowned. "That looks painful."

Lola held up the piercing cannula and batted her eyelashes. "It only hurts until the pain goes away."

This time, I grabbed Andrew's arm and pulled him with me toward the back door of the shop. "Is she really going to pierce his nipple?"

I put my hand on the lock, and before I could pull the door open, Gabe's cry rang out from cubicle two. "Ow! Jesus H. Christ!"

Andrew's mouth fell open and I nodded. "That would be a yes," I said. Andrew paled a little, so I opened the door for him. "After you."

FOUR

I PULLED THE DOOR SHUT BEHIND ME AND HEADED UP the external stairs that led to my place. I was used to the fire escape stairs. Most people probably thought it was a piss-poor entrance to someone's apartment, but it worked for me. I started up the stairs and heard Andrew climb up behind me. "It's okay if you want to check out my arse."

He stopped. "Do you say that to all the guys you bring up here?"

I laughed and looked back down at him. "Only the really hot ones."

He shook his head and didn't say anything else until I'd unlocked my door and walked inside my place. The truth was, I didn't bring any of my clients up here. I usually opted to do the whole getting-acquainted thing in a café or at their place. It put a buffer between my personal and professional life. I didn't know why I'd offered to bring Andrew into my home. I just didn't know.

My flat, or apartment as the Americans called it, was a small one-bedroom place. But the kitchen and bathroom were good, the combined living and dining area was long, and a huge window framed the far wall out onto Abbott Kinney Boulevard. When the sun went down, the nightlife of LA lit my living room, and during the day the sunlight was perfect for reading. Which was why there was a big papasan chair in front of the window. Near the window I had makeshift bookcases filled with mostly second-hand books. Actually, most things in my place were second-hand, scored from thrift stores or vintage markets, but somehow, when all put together, it worked.

"Nice place," he said, looking around. He nodded. "If there was a magazine called *Retro-Vintage-Bachelor Living,* this would be on the cover."

I laughed. "Emilio and Daniela used to live here," I told him. "They renovated the kitchen and bathroom while they were here, so it's pretty good. They moved out when Daniela's mum got sick; they wanted her to live with them but she couldn't manage the stairs."

Andrew nodded. "They seem like nice people." He said it like it was a question.

I stared at him for a long moment. "Even though they're covered in tattoos?"

His eyes shot to mine. "No, that's not what I said. I said they seem like nice people, given I've met them for a whole twenty seconds."

"You won't find more decent people," I told him. "Regardless of what they wear on their skin."

"I don't have anything against tattoos," he said. "Or the people that have them."

"Good," I said. "Because you and Emilio would get on really well. You're both artists, you both draw for a living. Only your drawing board doesn't move or bleed."

He conceded with a smile. "True."

I was glad the tension was gone. I didn't want to have to give him the "people with tattoos are people too" speech. He didn't seem the kind of guy who would be prejudiced against anyone for anything. Not that I knew him *that* well, but he seemed genuine. And it had been a while since I'd worked with someone who was.

In the short silence between us, he walked directly over to the vinyl record player. It was in a big wooden cabinet with a hinged lid that opened up to where the turntable was. "My grandparents had one of these," he said. He was smiling again. "Does it work?"

I walked over to it and stood beside him. I nodded to the vinyl record covers on the bookcase. "Yep."

"What have you got?" he asked, though he didn't wait for an answer. He simply helped himself to look. He flipped through them, considering each one. "Rather eclectic collection."

"Yeah," I agreed. "Everything from the Ramones to Billie Holiday."

He stopped flipping and slowly pulled out the record that had made him stop. "Can I play this?"

I nodded and smiled when I saw which one it was. It was a compilation of blues and jazz: Otis Redding, Bill Withers, Percy Sledge, Miles Davis, and Aretha Franklin. Andrew slid the record out of the cover like it was the most precious thing in the world, then carefully put the needle on the vinyl. The room filled with that familiar, perfect crackle that only vinyl gave, and "Ain't No Sunshine" started to play.

Andrew closed his eyes, lost in the music, and a slow smile spread across his face. He whispered, "It's incredible."

"So much is lost with modern music," I said quietly. He

looked at me then, so I explained. "I mean, I like contemporary music, but this—" I paused as Bill Withers sang. "—this is classic."

Andrew smiled at me, then shook his head disbelievingly. "So you curl up in the sun with a book while you listen to vinyl records?"

"Some days," I said. "Some days I use my iPod and belt out the Top 20. Depends what I'm in the mood for."

"What do your playlists look like?" he asked, genuinely interested.

I pulled out my phone, selected the music, and handed it to him. "Have a look." I left him to it, walked over to my dining table, and opened my laptop.

He took his time scrolling. "I've not heard of half of these," he said, his brow furrowed.

"Most of them are Aussie bands."

He made a thoughtful face. "I'll have to check them out when I get home."

"You can listen to them now if you want."

"I'd prefer to listen to this." He smiled as Otis Redding started to sing.

"So you play classical piano, but you like jazz?"

"Yes."

"What sheet music is on your piano right now?"

He grinned at me. "'Yesterdays' by Art Tatum."

I blinked. "Who?"

"Just the best jazz funk pianist to ever live."

"So wait," I said, putting my hands up. "You learned classical, but you play jazz?" He nodded sheepishly. "And you said you weren't cool? Or interesting? Jesus, Andrew. If there was a magazine called *Sexy and Cool Cartoonographers Who Play Jazz Funk Piano and Watch Stanley Kubrick Films*, you'd be on the cover. Of every issue."

He laughed, long and loud, and his cheeks tinted pink. Then he slid my phone back across the table to me and sat down in the seat next to mine. I'd typed Eli's name into Facebook to see who or what came up. There were a few, so I scrolled down the list.

"That's him there," Andrew said.

I let my finger hover over the icon. "Have you checked out his wall lately?"

Andrew shook his head. "No."

I clicked on his picture and Andrew looked away from the screen. "Everything okay?" I asked him.

"Yeah," he said, looking at me, but avoiding the laptop. "I just don't want to see if he's…"

"If he's posted pictures of himself with someone else?"

Andrew nodded. "I hadn't thought about that until you asked me if he was seeing someone else." Then he shook his head and narrowed his eyes. "And here I am trying to bait him into coming back to me. Kinda sad, huh?"

"No," I said gently. "Above all, you want answers. And that's what we're doing."

"Getting answers?"

"Yep."

"That I may or may not like to hear."

I sighed. "It's a possibility," I told him. "You might not like what he has to say, but wouldn't you be better off knowing?"

He nodded.

I scrolled down Eli's timeline. "He really should change his security settings." I could, as a complete stranger, see almost everything about him. Other people had tagged him in memes or jokes. He'd made a few posts over the last few weeks. "He never mentioned moving out or your separation," I said, and only then did Andrew look at the screen.

But then, posted earlier in the week, he was tagged in a conversation about this weekend. "Who's Terri Santos?"

"Eli works with her. They're friends though. We'd go out with her sometimes."

"She says here they're going to the Basement for her birthday drinks and asked him if he wanted to join them."

"When?"

"Tonight, at eight."

"What did he say?" he asked, as he leaned in to read the post and comments in question.

I paraphrased Eli's reply. "Said he doesn't want to be sick for work tomorrow, but he might call in for a few."

Andrew looked from the screen to me, and I realised how close we were. His blue eyes had flecks of grey in them, which I'd not noticed before. He was so good looking, he smelled damn good, and he was so, so close.

"What are you thinking?" he asked.

Shit. "About what?" *Because what I was thinking about was sliding my hand along your jaw and kissing you. I bet you taste as good as you smell...*

"About Eli, of course."

"Oh, right, yes. Of course," I said, shaking my head of the stupid thoughts I'd just had. "We should go. You and me, to the Basement, tonight."

"Oh."

"If we want Eli to see you on a date with another guy, then we need to actually go out."

"On a date?"

"We know it's not real, but he won't."

He seemed to think this over, as though he was wondering if he wanted to do this at all. "Okay."

"Are you sure you want to do this?"

He looked at me with those soul-seeing blue-grey eyes. "Well, yeah."

He didn't sound very convinced, and I wasn't sure why that pleased me. We had hours before our first public outing in front of our intended target audience, but even so, we had some work to do. I wasn't sure which of us would struggle more. Normally I could get close to my clients and not think anything of it. Andrew was different. I looked at my watch. "Well, we have a while yet, but maybe we should practice a little?"

"Practice?"

"Yeah," I swallowed hard. "You know, our story for the public, how we met, holding hands, that kind of thing."

He blanched. "Oh."

"I'm not that repulsive, am I?" I half-joked, half-not.

Andrew blushed. "Ah, no. Definitely not." He stood up from the table and walked into my small kitchen. He leaned against the counter and folded his arms, then unfolded them as though it was a habit he was trying to break, then shoved his hands in his pockets instead. He cleared his throat and asked, "So, what do we tell people about how we met?"

"Your sister and my best friend met at a wedding last weekend," I said

"Well, technically they did," he said, confused.

"Exactly. It's best to stick to the truth as much as possible," I explained. "That way, if Eli runs into Sarah in the street or the store and puts her on the spot with questions, no one has to lie."

"I really don't think he'll buy it," he said quietly. "This whole you and me thing."

"Why not?"

He stared at me like I'd missed the obvious.

"Don't start with that *but look at me* crap," I said with a smirk. "Unless you have a problem with tattoos and Eli knows that. Is that what you mean?" I showed him how my ink never went past my wrists. I had no tattoos on my hands or my neck, or my chest or back for that matter. I was strictly a sleeves-only guy. "Because I can wear a long-sleeved shirt and he won't even be able to tell."

Andrew shook his head. "No, don't change a thing," he said quietly. Then he shrugged one shoulder. "It's just the whole, you know, you're trendy and I'm not thing."

"Oh yeah, that's right," I said standing up. "I'm just some random guy on page four of *Gay and Trendy*, and you're the cover model of *Cool*."

He laughed at that and shook his head at me. "You know what I mean."

"No I don't. But you know what? It doesn't matter. If he is inclined to think us being together is out of character, then at least we know we have his attention."

He considered this. "True."

I stood up and walked to stand in front of him. I was closer than what would probably be considered polite, but that was my point. I held out my hand between us, palm up. He obviously didn't know what I meant, so I explained. "Your hand?"

Slowly, he put his hand in mine. I held it, feeling the warmth and smooth skin of his palm, then traced my thumb over his knuckles. Then I held his hand in both of mine and gave it a squeeze. "This okay?" I asked.

He nodded.

"So when we're out together, if I grab your hand, you won't pull it away?"

He shook his head, and he whispered, "No."

I could feel his body heat, I could feel his nervousness. Or maybe it was mine. Either way, the air between us was electric. Sure, I'd been close with other clients—held hands, danced, even kissed—but it was no more than acting. I was playing a role, no more, no less.

So why was I nervous? Maybe it had been too long between drinks, so to speak. Maybe I needed to go out and let loose. And maybe when this job was done, that's exactly what I'd do.

I didn't know why Andrew was different. He was interesting, sure. He was smart and made me laugh. At first I thought he was just humble about his job and his musical talents, but the more I got to know him, the more I realised he wasn't humble at all. He was oblivious.

I had to wonder what the fuck was wrong with Eli to want to walk away from him.

It was then I realised he was holding my hand as much as I was holding his. He didn't just let his hand sit limp in mine. He ran his thumb along the side of my hand and his fingers kind of gripped onto mine. It was comforting and warm, and above all, it just felt really nice.

I swallowed down the unexpected lump in my throat. "And if we have to dance?"

It took him a moment to answer. I wasn't sure if he was aware of the static between us or if it was just me. "Oh, I don't dance."

"Okay, fair enough," I said. I was okay with that. Some people didn't like to dance, and that was fine. "But what if there's loud music and I need to lean in close?" I asked. My voice was husky from trying to whisper and getting all breathy instead.

He blinked quickly and licked his bottom lip. We were still holding hands, so I took one hand each in mine and spread his arms out at the sides. I leaned in slow, feeling his warmth but not quite touching, and ignoring how good he smelled, I put my lips to his ear. "This okay?"

He nodded, and I'm pretty sure he didn't breathe.

I pulled back so I could see his face but still kept hold of his hands. "If he's watching us, I might lean in to talk in your ear. But it will only be to get his attention."

He cleared his throat. "And that worked with other guys?"

"Other clients?" I clarified. There was a distinct difference between guys I liked and guys I worked with. "It usually works, yes."

He let out a deep breath. "Oh, okay."

"And I'll only kiss you if we need it to seal the deal," I told him. "Kinda like the make or break kiss. He either won't care, or he'll let me know he didn't appreciate my touching you. But if I do kiss you, you'll need to trust me that it's because Eli's watching and warring with himself about coming over. Just go along with it."

His eyes were wide. "Oh."

I almost laughed. "We don't need to practice kissing," I added. "Unless you want to."

He snorted, and a blush crept up his neck. "Ah, I think I'm familiar with how it works."

"Though I've only had to kiss one client once. Most of the time a well-placed hand and whispering in your ear will do the trick. Like this," I said, letting go of his hand so I could put my hand on his waist. On his hard, well-defined waist. "Jesus, what you got going on under that shirt?"

He blanched. "What?"

I gave his side a squeeze. "You're like ripped or something!"

He jumped and grabbed my hand with a laugh. "Ah!"

"You're ticklish?" I asked, laughing with him. "Good to know."

His cheeks were red, but he was still smiling, and the

serious mood between us was broken. I didn't know whether to be grateful or disappointed. I shook myself out and took a deep breath. "Okay, serious again."

He looked at me weirdly. "What was it like when you kissed that guy?"

"My client?"

He nodded.

"To be honest, it was awkward," I admitted. "I didn't really like him, so it wasn't natural, if that's what you mean?"

"You didn't like him?"

"I mean, he wasn't my type."

He nodded. "Did it work?" he asked. "Did it get his ex's attention?"

"It sure did. Like I said, I'm good at what I do."

He bit his bottom lip and looked away. Eventually he nodded, as though he'd come to some conclusion in his head.

"If you want to draw the line at something, please just say," I told him. "If me kissing you makes you uncomfortable, you have to tell me. Ultimately it all comes down to you. You're the boss here."

He took a while to answer, and I worried for a second he'd say no to the possibility of me kissing him, or even touching him. I didn't know why that bothered me. Probably because he was so cute and he smelled so good and his lips looked so damn kissable...

"It's fine," he answered. Then he shook his head and chuckled nervously. "My God, this is weird."

I breathed a sigh of relief, unable to stop from smiling. "Only if we let it get weird."

He shoved his hands in his pockets again. "So, what do we do for the next few hours?"

There was absolutely no reason for him to be here for the next few hours at least. If it were anyone else, I would have bid him farewell and told him I'd call past his place at seven. But this was different. I didn't know why it was different. It just was. So instead of telling him to leave, I said, "How 'bout you pick another record for us to listen to?"

Then he had to go and pick Jeff Buckley's live LP, and I knew right then and there I was in trouble.

FIVE

He sat on my papasan chair like a cat in the sun and listened to the vinyl recording of my most favourite album. I sat on the sofa with my laptop, trying to find out what I could on Eli Masterson, but truthfully, I was just watching Andrew.

"So, Eli works eight till four, Monday to Friday?" I asked, trying to get my mind on the job.

"Shush."

I blinked. He just fucking shushed me. "Really?"

He grinned at me. "You can't talk while this is playing." Then he tilted his head a little and listened to Jeff Buckley sing. "Show a little respect to the man."

"Oh, I respect Mr Buckley." I threw a cushion at him.

He caught the cushion and sank down a little in the papasan chair as he laughed, curling up all comfortable-like and smiling, still reading over the album cover and looking as though he belonged there. As though I wanted him to belong there. And that realisation startled me.

"What?" he asked. "You look like you swallowed a pill."

I shook my head. "Nothing. No, it's all good." Trying to get my heart rate back to normal, I looked back at the laptop screen, just as the song "Hallelujah" started. And like always, it made me stop. I took a deep breath and just listened.

When I looked over at Andrew, he was smiling at me. "I see what you mean. It's a great song. I don't know about perfect—"

"Shush!" I said back to him.

He chuckled again and waited until the song was played out. "Yes, Eli works eight till four, Monday through Friday."

Right. Eli. Shit. "Does he play any sport on weekends? Soccer, football, tennis?"

Andrew shook his head. "Um, no."

"I just wondered if there was somewhere else we could just turn up to, that's all." I sighed. "Does he have a favourite grocery store? A café? Bookstore? Park?"

Andrew rattled off a few of Eli's other haunts and what he did in his free time. From what I understood, they rarely did anything together, and Eli seemed rather boring. It was hard to explain, but for all Andrew told me about Eli, the less I knew about him.

"What did you guys used to do on a Sunday afternoon?" I asked. "Didn't go to a jazz bar with friends?"

He shook his head slowly. "Nope."

"Why not?" I asked. "You love jazz."

"I guess we never got around to it," he said with a shrug.

"I think I need to talk to this Eli of yours."

He froze and his smile was gone. "Why?"

"To tell him to wake up to himself," I said jokingly, although I wasn't really joking at all. "Because that's the first place I'd take you."

Andrew laughed at that, and his cheeks tinted pink. "God, I thought you meant you were gonna knock on his door or something."

"Well, no. I wasn't going to. I mean I could, but I prefer no contact with the target, thanks."

"The target?"

"Yep."

"You make it sound like it's some covert operation or something."

"It is! We have code words and everything."

"Code words?"

"Well, phrases, but yes," I told him. "Like if he approaches you in a bar, I'd say, 'I'll just wait outside,' which is code for *good luck*. Or if the target is having sex with some other dude in the bathrooms, I'll say, 'Shots of tequila are on me,' which is code for *game over*."

He made a face. "I hate tequila."

I found myself smiling at him. "Me too. But I think you missed the point."

He laughed again, which told me he didn't miss the point at all. He turned the LP cover over in his hand. "How did Jeff Buckley die?"

"Um..." Random subject change, but okay. "He drowned. Walked out into the Mississippi, fully clothed, singing Led Zeppelin's 'Whole Lotta Love', and never came out."

Andrew blinked. "Jeez."

"Why?"

"I never knew, that's all."

Just then, his phone beeped. He fished it out of his pocket and read the screen. "It's Sarah," he said.

So while he had a text conversation with his sister, I did another quick Facebook scroll on Eli, his friends, family— anything that might strike me as odd. There was nothing out of the ordinary. There were also no pictures of him with Andrew. Granted, he didn't post a lot, or often, but still. I'd have thought he would have at least mentioned having a boyfriend, let alone a live-in boyfriend. Not to even mention the fact they were supposed to be engaged. Or even the break-up. People were forever posting break-ups on Facebook for sympathy and to notify their list of friends that they were back on the market. There was no mention of Andrew at all.

So then I looked up Andrew.

Andrew's timeline was mostly people tagging him in jokes or memes. There were a few posts from Sarah. They seemed like nice people. Nothing religious or political, nothing offensive. Some holiday pictures and, after scrolling a while, I found a picture of Andrew and Sarah. It was an old photo, when Andrew and Sarah were little, in what looked like some family holiday. A happy family, a perfect family even.

A pang of sadness pierced my chest, and I quickly exited out, just as Andrew put his phone away. Thankful for the distraction, I asked, "Everything okay?"

"Oh yeah," he said, rolling his eyes. "Mom's invited her to a lunch thing next month and Sarah just gave me the heads up that if she has to go, so do I."

"Sounds fun."

He scoffed. "If by fun you mean boring as hell, then you'd be correct."

He had no idea just how good a family lunch sounded. He stared at me for a long second, then reached over to put the album cover on top of the record player. "Come on," he said, standing up. "Let's go."

I slowly closed my laptop. "Uh, where exactly are we going?"

"You're going to buy me my first Jeff Buckley album."

I grinned at him. "Oh, am I?"

"Yes, you are. Unless you want to give me that one." He pointed to my record player.

"Like hell. That's my favourite."

"That's what I thought," he said, walking to the door. He turned back to look at me—where I hadn't moved from—and clapped his hands together. "Look alive, Spencer."

"Alright," I said, collecting my wallet and keys. I quickly grabbed two bottled waters out of my fridge and handed one to him as we walked out the door. "Are you always so pushy?"

He laughed, and those little lines crinkled the corners of his eyes, and the sun gave a warmth to his skin. He went down the stairs first and waited for me to get to the bottom. I guessed he was unsure of which direction to go. I pointed my thumb to the tattoo shop's dead bolted door. "Can't access the shop from the outside, so we'll have to go around," I nodded toward the end of the building, and we settled into a comfortable stride next to each other.

"I assume there's a music store around here somewhere," he said as we neared the street.

"There's a few," I told him. "Did you want a CD or an LP? I could have just downloaded it for you if that would have been easier."

"LP, for sure."

"Do you have a record player?"

"Well, no. But I think I'll have to get one. I would imagine jazz and blues from vinyl would be incredible."

I grinned at him. "I've created a monster!"

"You can't just play classic vinyl albums to a music lover and not expect him to want it."

I grinned. "True."

We walked the two blocks, the banter between us never stopping. He talked with his hands when he explained things, which I found to be rather endearing, and I'm pretty sure I hadn't stopped smiling since we left my place. We tossed our empty water bottles into a recycling bin before I led him down a side alley off the boulevard and stood in front of the door to the music shop. "Before we go in, you must promise me something."

He was suddenly serious. "What?"

"This place is special, and thus, must remain a secret."

"Thus?"

"It's a word."

"That no one has used in two hundred years."

"Not true. I just used it now."

He laughed. "Okay, so I'm not supposed to tell anyone I came here?"

"Nope. It's like Vegas."

"As in 'What happens in Vegas, stays in Vegas'? Really?"

"Yes, really." I nodded. "It's too awesome to be popular."

"Isn't that redundant to their business profitability?"

"Possibly. But it's completely old-school indie. I think the owner was a pot-smoking surfer from the sixties and has principles against corporations, though I've never asked him. Anyway, if too many people know about it, then it becomes mainstream. And that would ruin it."

He frowned at me. "Then it's not like Vegas. It's more like *Fight Club*."

I laughed and bowed my head. "Ah, Grasshopper. You have passed the test. You may enter." He beamed, and I opened the door with a laugh.

He stepped inside. "Okay, wow."

The music shop was like a tribute to the 70s. Instead of neon lights and flashing digital screens, there were band posters and vintage T-shirts pinned to the walls. And rows and rows of vinyl records.

"Cool, huh?"

He nodded slowly, and still looking at the rows of albums, he said, "Where do I start?"

"This way," I said, leading him to the folk section.

"They're categorized by genre, then alphabetically." I found the B section. "Here. Jeff Buckley."

He flicked through some of the covers. "Which one would I like?" he asked, more to himself than to me.

"His *Live from Sin-é* album," I told him. "He covered Billie Holiday and Nina Simone. You'd love it."

I took over looking through the covers, and when I looked up, he was staring at me. I mean, we were standing shoulder to shoulder, rifling through vintage records, and he was staring right at me. "What?"

He quickly turned back to the album covers. "Nothing." He shook his head. "You can look through these. I'll just... check out the record players," he mumbled so quietly, I barely heard him. And he walked off to look at the old record players and turntables.

Odd. But, figuring I didn't exactly know him that well, it was hard to gauge what was weird behaviour or not. I found the album I was after and pulled out the sleeve. The vinyl looked unscratched, so with a smile, I slid the album back into the cover and followed Andrew over to the far wall. "Found it," I told him.

"Oh, cool, thanks," he said. He was clearly distracted by the record players, because he didn't look at me. "Which of these do you think?"

They were only table top units, not whole cabinets like mine. He seemed undecided between two. "I think the black one. It has speakers built in," I told him. "And it'll match the frames on your wall and your piano."

He smiled at me. "True."

"Now," I said, looking around. "It's only fair that you pick an album for me."

He looked around the store and blinked. "Oh."

"Not something you'd think I'd like, but something you'd

pick for yourself."

He headed straight for the jazz section. He flipped through covers, pulling faces at some, frowning at others, and some got a look of disgust. But then he pulled out one record, read the back of it for the song list, and he smiled. He held it up for me to see. It was called *Jazz Piano: Funk and Fusion*. To say I was surprised was an understatement. "The cover looks like a bad 70s porn movie."

He laughed but quickly looked around to see who might have heard me. "Well, the cover isn't great, but the songs are."

He handed it to me, and I read over the names of songs and artists I'd never heard before. "You'd listen to this?" I asked.

"I would."

"*Jazz Piano: Funk and Fusion?*"

He chuckled. "Don't knock it until you hear it."

I exhaled through puffed out cheeks. "Okay, you're the boss."

I took the albums to the counter and the guy there gave an approving nod. His huge afro didn't move. "Excellent choice," he said, looking at Andrew's pick.

"See?" Andrew said, nudging me with his elbow. "Told you it was good."

I rolled my eyes but then said to the guy behind the counter, "And the black record player, thanks."

Andrew pulled out his wallet, but I handed the sales guy my card. "I'm paying."

"You can't do that!" Andrew objected.

"I just did," I said. I had no idea *why* I did. But it felt right. The cashier finalized the sale, handed me back my card and I handed the records to Andrew. "You can carry them," I told him, picking up the record player.

He was quiet for half the walk back to my place. "I can't believe you did that," he said.

"It was no big deal," I replied.

He made a face I couldn't interpret, and when we got to the tattoo shop, he stopped. "Thank you," he said, his hand on the door. "It was very kind, and I didn't mean to sound ungrateful."

"You didn't sound ungrateful," I told him. "More shocked that someone would do something like that for you."

He bit his lip. "No one has."

"I really need to speak to this Eli of yours," I said jokingly. "Because that is a crying shame."

Without another word, he pushed on the door and held it open for me. I gave him a nod, "Thank you, kind sir." He rolled his eyes.

"Hey, here they are," Emilio called. He was leaning over the front counter with a pen in hand, working on some tracing paper. He stood up straight and stretched his back. "Whatcha got there?"

"Record player," I said. "Andrew didn't have one."

Andrew held the two LPs like they were a shield. "Spencer bought it for me."

Emilio laughed, but there was a curious look in his eyes, which I very astutely ignored. "Well, plug it in and let's listen," he said.

I put the record player on the coffee table and took the cord out from the back. "Well, I bought one LP for Andrew and one for me."

"He got a Jeff Buckley for me," Andrew said. He was nervous but making an effort.

I plugged the player in. "And Andrew chose some *Jazz Piano: Funk and Crap* for me."

Andrew narrowed his eyes at me. "It's not crap."

"Oh, is that what I said? I meant to say *Jazz Piano: Funk and Fusion*. Crap must have just slipped out."

Grinning, Emilio told Andrew, "He gets away with saying shit like that because of his Australian accent."

I scoffed. "Like you can talk. You get all suave with your Spanish when you're sweet talking Daniela."

Emilio gave me a shit-eating grin, and Daniela called out from the back cubicle. "And it works, every time."

Emilio replied to her, something in Spanish about tonight and the rest I chose not to follow. But by the way Andrew blushed, I'd say he understood every word. He cleared his throat and handed me the two records. Figuring I'd be polite, I chose the Jazz record and slid the vinyl out of the cover, putting it on the turntable and carefully lowering the tonearm.

The familiar crackle sounded, then a piano intro played. It reminded me of those old movies of a Ray Charles type, sitting in a dive bar in New Orleans. I was intrigued. Then a double bass thrummed in, followed by what sounded like a whole brass section. "Hey this isn't bad," I told him.

Andrew looked a little smug and a lot cute, so I pretended to be grossly interested in the album cover. And when I looked up again, Andrew was standing over near the counter, watching Emilio draw.

It was easy to forget, with one being tattooed and a little rough around the edges and the other being clean cut and Ivy League that they were both artists.

I should have realised that they would have a lot in common.

I left the music playing and joined them at the counter. Andrew was just watching as Emilio drew waves and the sun, and after a while Emilio looked up at him. "It's very good," Andrew said.

Emilio shrugged the compliment off. "Thanks."

"Andrew's an artist too," I reminded him.

Emilio looked at Andrew, like he'd forgotten that too. "Cool. What do you draw?"

"Character story boards," he said like it wasn't remarkable. He couldn't take his eyes off the stencil paper. "Your freehand technique is incredible."

"Freehand is what I do," Emilio said. "It's easier on paper than on skin, but sometimes to get the rise and fall of the body, I need to freehand directly onto the skin."

"Jesus," Andrew whispered. "I couldn't ever do that."

"Character story boards sounds pretty cool though," Emilio said. He grabbed a slip of tracing paper and pushed a pen to him. "Show me what you can do."

Andrew looked at me, the corners of his lips pulled down. Then he smiled and put pen to paper. In what was seriously no more than a few swipes of the pen and an endearing pout as he drew, he pushed the piece of paper out. It was very simplistic but equally identifiable. It was the head and shoulders of a guy, cartoon-like from a movie, but this guy had his hair styled up, short on the sides, and stubble on his jaw. But it was the suspenders I wore on the day I met him that gave it away.

He'd drawn me.

Emilio burst out laughing and offered Andrew his hand in a brother's type of handshake.

I scowled at them, feigning offense, when really it was pretty freakin' cool. "Oh, look! It's the guy from page four of *Trendy Living*."

Andrew laughed and snatched back the paper, and above the little guy he drew the words *Trendy Living*, like it was a magazine cover. He wrote Spencer Cohen underneath it. "There. Now he's on the cover."

I laughed, and before I could snatch up the drawing, Emilio took it. "This is going on our Wall of Fame." He pinned it among the other photos of tattoos.

Just then the door opened and two women came in and smiled at Emilio. "Just finishing up the drawing now," he told them. "Take a seat. Won't be a minute."

One of the ladies bopped her head. "Cool music!"

Andrew whacked my arm. "Told you."

I laughed but said, "Come on. We'd better leave Emilio to it."

"You can stay if you like," one of the ladies said suggestively. She looked between me and Andrew. "You both can."

Figuring it was a good time to test him on public displays of affection, I slid my arm around Andrew's waist. "Sorry, ladies. We have *things* that need doing."

Andrew blushed, and he might have held his breath, but he didn't flinch.

"Oh," she said, getting the point. "Shame."

"Not for me," Andrew said, shocking the hell outta me.

I burst out laughing just as Daniela came out from the back. She looked at me with a weird smile on her face, and as Andrew and I collected the record player and the two LPs, I noticed Daniela give Emilio a questioning look. I ignored it, and thankfully neither one of them said anything. Not in front of Andrew anyway. I knew I'd probably get roasted later.

Andrew really was a surprising man. His appearance said he should be straight-laced, a good all-American boy, mild mannered, shy, and even a bit nerdy. But his sense of humour, his taste in movies and music, and his intelligence made him intriguing to me. He would come out with the least expected comments and lines, and I was really starting to think that Eli must be fucking crazy to have walked away from him.

"Aren't we going this way?" Andrew asked, nodding toward the back of the shop.

I walked to the front door. "Nope. We're going to your place. Buses are this way."

Andrew shrugged but didn't move. "Well, you can catch the bus if you want, but I drove. My car is this way." He pointed to the back of the store.

Emilio laughed, and I flipped him off. Raising my chin, I walked past Andrew. "This way then."

"Bye, boys," Daniela said. "Lola said she'd call you tomorrow."

"Thanks," I said, giving her a smirk on the way out. I held the back door open for Andrew. "You could have just said you drove."

He smiled as he walked out into the sunshine and over to a BMW parked in the lot behind the row of shops, where we'd walked past earlier. "You didn't even say 'Hey, that's my car' when we walked right by it."

He unlocked it and opened the driver's door. "Can't go telling you all my secrets in two days, can I?"

"The fact you drive a car isn't exactly a secret." I put the record player on the backseat, and got in the front passenger seat of his immaculately clean car.

"Well, you never asked me if I drove," he said, shifting the gearstick into reverse. "What if Eli had asked you about my car? You'd have failed."

"I would have told him I was too busy letting you fuck me in the backseat to notice what kind of car it was."

He grinded the gears, and his mouth fell open.

I burst out laughing. "Just kidding. We'd never fit back there. Reverse cowboy on this seat, however..."

He narrowed his eyes at me, put the car into first, and

swung it around neatly. "Do you always go for the shock value?"

"Sometimes. Sometimes it's just funny. Like now."

He shook his head at me and pulled the car out onto the street. "Was that funny?"

"Yep. And it also told me something without having to ask."

"What's that?"

"You didn't correct me when I assumed you'd top me," I said, going for casual, though my dick wasn't casual about it at all.

"Ah, veto." He cleared his throat and blushed a palette of reds. "Veto, veto, veto."

I laughed. "Fair enough. But I can tell you're totally imagining it right now."

He glared at me.

I pointed to the road. "Watch the road. Jesus!"

He did, thankfully. "Would you like to drive?"

I snorted. "Hell no. Wrong side of the car, wrong side of the road for me."

He grumbled something that sounded a lot like 'Freakin' Australians' as he weaved in and out of traffic. I had to admit. He was a good driver. And his car was very nice.

"I haven't driven a car since I got here," I admitted.

"Not at all?"

"Nope. I either bus it or walk. I live central to everywhere I want to be. I kinda miss it though, to be honest."

He considered this for a while. "I was only joking before, but I could pull over if you want to actually drive?"

"No," I said, smiling at him. "I'd rather not crash your car on our second date."

"Date?"

"Well, you know what I mean. For all intents and

purposes, and if Eli asks, then yes. It's a date." This seemed to shock him, so I added, "Don't panic though, I don't expect you to put out on the second date."

He shook his head at me. "You are insufferable."

I hummed contentedly. "Thank you. You did well back there, by the way. When I put my arm around you. You played it cool."

"I uh, I wasn't expecting it."

"I wasn't expecting you to tell that lady it wasn't a shame for you that I was gay."

He checked his rear vision mirror and changed lanes. "Yeah well, that annoys me. Saying it's a shame someone is gay." He scowled. "It's disrespectful."

"It is," I agreed.

"I hope Emilio didn't mind me saying that to his customers."

"Not at all. Emilio has no qualms with putting rude people in their place."

"He's very good at drawing freehand," he said. "It just surprised me. I guess I've never thought of tattoo artists as *artists*."

"He sure is. Except his drawing board is the human body."

That made him smile. "What are we doing back at my place anyway?" he asked. "Aren't we supposed to be going out tonight?"

"Yep, we sure are. We need to get your record player all set up because you haven't listened to Jeff Buckley sing Nina Simone."

He pulled the car into a spot not far from his house, and he just sat there for a second like he wanted to say something but wasn't sure if he should. In the end, he said, "Sounds good."

He was a bit reserved after that. Kinda like he was the

very first day I met him in the café. God, was that really just two days ago? He seemed to have a defensive wall up now, the kind that made his smile not quite right and his conversation a little stilted. He put the record player on his dining table. "Wanna plug it in?" I asked.

He wiped his hands on his trousers. "Maybe later. Want a bottle of water?"

"Uh, sure." I gave him my best smile. I don't know why that bothered me so much and why I wanted more than anything to right whatever I did that was wrong. He offered me a drink but genuinely looked upset by something. I wanted to ask him if he was okay, but I didn't want him to tell me the whole deal was off. I didn't want to stop spending time with him. So I pretended there was nothing wrong and charted the mood back into safer waters. "Have any movies?"

What the fuck was I doing? My brain was telling me to leave. My stupid heart was telling my stupid feet to stay right where they were and telling my stupid mouth to ask him stupid questions.

"Ah, sure," he called out from the kitchen. "In the cabinet underneath the TV. Or there's Netflix."

I opened the cabinet, wanting to see what his movie collection said about him. I smiled when I saw the first DVD. *How to Train Your Dragon.* I pulled it out and held it up as he walked back into the room.

He smiled a genuine smile. "The second one's in there too," he said. "I thought you said you've seen the first, not the second."

I opened the case and slid the disc into the machine. "I have seen this one. But we need to watch them in order."

He chuckled and plonked himself on the sofa, looking more relaxed. Whatever was bothering him just moments ago seemed forgotten and that made me happier than it probably should have. I collected the remote controls from their neat little row underneath the large flat screen and handed them to him when I sat at the other end of the sofa. I was going to plant myself right next to him but figured I wouldn't risk him freaking out on me again. He gave me the bottled water. "Thanks."

He pressed some buttons and the movie started, but then he did something to his end of the sofa, and it slowly leaned back, becoming a recliner. "Hey," I said. "How do I do that?"

His lips curved upwards at the bottle he was drinking from. "There's a button on the side."

I found the button and the footrest slowly came up, and the back automatically reclined. "Oh man, I need to get me one of these."

"My sister told me it was a waste of money. But it was the best decision ever."

"I can see why." God it was comfy. "Okay, so you have to tell me about anything in the movie that you've drawn for promo work."

He smiled. "Okay."

"What's your favourite to work on?" I asked. "The humans or the dragons?"

"Dragons."

"Which one?"

"Toothless."

"Of course."

"Is that a problem?"

I laughed. "No. There'd be something wrong if he wasn't. He's the cutest, for sure."

Andrew laughed at that. "He is. He's very cat-like to draw."

We watched in silence for a while. "Have you worked on anything so far?" I asked. "I want to see your work."

He tossed the DVD cover at me and flicked up one eyebrow before turning back to the movie. I looked at the cover, not quite getting what his point was. Then it hit me. *Oh my God.* "You drew the cover?"

"I was thinking I was going to have to hit you over the head with it," he said with a laugh. "I worked on it, yes. It's not just *my* work. It takes a huge team of people."

I shook my head in disbelief. "You worked on the freakin' cover? That is so cool! You should totally own that. How come you don't tell everyone?"

"Because I'm not a dick about it."

I snorted. "I would *so* be a dick about it."

He laughed at that. "Well, there are enough name droppers and celebrity wannabes in this city without me adding to them."

"And you know what?" I asked. "That's what I like about you."

His lips twitched as he fought a smile. "Thanks." He looked back to the movie. "And you too. You're not some social-ladder climber either. It's nice to find that in this town."

His words made my heart trip over, which caught me off guard. Kinda like being smashed side-on by a front-row forward in a rugby match.

He looked at me and bit his lip, and I could almost see his mind ticking over. Then he smiled. "I want to show you something." He jumped off the sofa and waited for me to press the button so the automatic recliner got back into position. He raised one eyebrow at me. "You could just climb off, you know."

"No way," I said. "I still have the scars from my Nanna's boot up my arse for jumping off her recliner when I was about six. I have dutifully righted every reclining chair I've ever sat in before getting up off it since."

He let out a laugh but nodded toward the stairs. "Come on, it's up here."

I followed him, gaining an awesome view of his arse on the way. He stopped at the end doorway, but I could see inside. His bed, a high queen-size with a solid wooden frame, was perfectly made. The cover and matching pillows were black and gold, and I knew without touching them they were expensive. And soft. "If you just wanted me in your bedroom, you only had to ask," I joked.

Only I wasn't really joking. I wouldn't mind spending some time in his room.

He walked in, over to another door. "In my closet actually."

"You want me in your walk-in robe?"

He stared at me, confused. "My what?"

Bloody Australianisms still tripped me up. "Ugh. Closet. Walk-in robe. Same thing. Seriously, you need to learn Australian to speak to me. And anyway, you really want to take me in your closet?" I shrugged. "I'm okay with kink."

He stopped with his hand on the door. "I don't have any *kinks*," he said. "Is it always about sex with you?"

"Not always," I admitted. "I'm rather partial to food and music too."

"In any particular order?"

"Nope. I like to change it up a little. Keep 'em guessing, ya know?"

He rolled his eyes and turned to the door. "I haven't really showed anyone these, but I think you might appreciate them."

I remembered how excited he was downstairs when he

obviously decided he wanted me to see whatever was inside, so I was curious as to what on earth it could be. He opened the door, and on the right side of the long walk-in closet were shelves and neatly hanging clothes. But on the left side was just a bare wall. Except it wasn't *just* a wall. There was a long, thin horizontal window above my head which was great for natural light, but covering the wall were frames of story boards. Boards he'd obviously drawn; some were black and white, some were coloured. Some were fully complete, some were outlines only.

"Oh wow," I whispered. Characters I recognised immediately from movies I'd seen, I couldn't take my eyes off them. "Andrew, they're incredible."

He grinned, almost with relief it seemed. Did he honestly think I wouldn't like them? "They're pretty cool."

"Cool?" I repeated. "They're amazing. You're amazing. I can't believe you drew these!" Embarrassment crept over his cheeks, but there was a dash of pride too. "Why aren't these on your living room wall with the Dragon ones?"

He looked them over and sighed. "I don't know. I guess I don't want my work to stare at me every day. It's not all that I am," he said quietly.

"Fair enough," I replied. "I can see your point. But seriously? These are incredible! Not even on your bedroom wall?"

He snorted out a laugh. "Not sure grown men would appreciate having cartoon characters looking." He cleared his throat. "If you know what I mean."

I scoffed at that. "Then you're clearly bringing the wrong guys home." I meant it as an off the cuff remark, but it made me wonder. "Did Eli like them?"

"Yeah. But I think he was kind of glad they were hidden. Like I said, no one's seen these."

"Well, I am impressed." I looked them over again. "Which is your favourite?"

His face lit up. "This one." He pointed to a full colour one of Marty, the zebra with a rainbow coloured afro from *Madagascar*. "He was fun to draw. Which one do you like?"

I pointed to one in particular of the two main characters from *Kung Fu Panda*. "The way it's just half an outline, with general body shapes. We can see who they are, but..."

"But what?"

"I like how it's open for interpretation. It could be them with their backs to us, walking off as a goodbye, or it could be them coming to life. You know, just the beginning."

When he didn't answer, I looked at him to find he was staring at me. He opened his mouth but then shook his head and decided not to say whatever it was he was struggling to say.

"Does that make sense?" I asked. "Or did I get it wrong?"

He swallowed hard, his eyes never left mine, and his voice was just a whisper. "Perfect sense. Thank you."

Suddenly the air in that walk-in closet was static. I wanted to reach out and touch him, to kiss him. God, I wanted to taste his mouth. But that's not what this was. I was here to help him get his ex back. Thankful for the reminder of what I was actually doing there, I looked up at the window and saw the colour of the sky. "It's uh—" I took a breath to collect myself. "it's getting late. We should eat before we go out, yeah?"

He took a step back and breathed out slowly. Which told me I wasn't imagining the electricity between us. "Uh yeah."

I turned around to face the clothes side of his wardrobe. "You know, I don't think I've ever seen a more neatly organised closet." Even the folded clothes were done to perfection.

He touched a random hanging shirt. "It's not like I haven't had a lot of spare time lately."

Oh right. Eli. And again, it came back to him. I was

starting to hate the guy, and I'd never even laid eyes on him. "Are any of these clothes his?"

Andrew's eyes narrowed a fraction. "No."

"That's a shame. I was hoping he might have left a shirt behind or something?"

"Why?"

"So I can wear it," I told him. "Just something else he might notice. We want to get a reaction from him, right?"

"I guess," he answered. Then he picked out a knitted vest, in the same argyle pattern as the sweater he was wearing, only it was blue and grey not blue and red. He held it up on the hanger. "He bought me this."

"Even better," I said with a smile. "Can I wear it?"

He blinked in surprise. "Okay."

I held it up to my shirt. "Does it match?"

"Um, not really."

He was right. It was a different shade of blue. I pulled a white long-sleeved, button-down shirt out by the hanger. "This'll fit me."

We were roughly the same height, but completely different builds. I was lean, he was solid, and from what I felt of his abs earlier, I'd say he was pretty damn fit. It was a shame he chose to cover it up with sweaters, no matter how cute they made him look.

I started to unbutton my shirt. "What are you doing?" he asked.

"Well, I can't wear your shirt over the top of mine." I got the last button undone and shucked out of it. "Don't worry, I'll pay to have them dry cleaned."

"It's not that," he said and cleared his throat. He tried not to look at me, but he seemed unable to help himself. I had no problems with him looking. "Your chest is bare."

"Hey," I said, deeply offended. "I have *some* chest hair." I patted down the fine fuzz.

He laughed, but he was blushing so hard even his ears turned pink. "No, I mean you don't have tattoos on your chest."

"Nope. Sleeves only." I looked down at my shoulders, where the ink stopped and bare skin started. "What? Does that surprise you?"

"Well, yeah. I just assumed you'd have them, well, everywhere." He was still blushing, and trying not to ogle me, and trying not to smile.

"Nah, not yet. Maybe one day. They're kind of addictive, but I like what I have so far." I slipped on his shirt and started to do the buttons up. "If I found the right one, I probably would."

He considered this, but didn't say anything.

When I had the shirt on, I lifted both arms out. "This fits me pretty well, actually. You have good taste in clothes."

He granted me a small smile. "Thanks."

I started to roll up the sleeve, but stopped. "Sleeves up or down?" I asked. "Do you want him to see them or not?"

"It's up to you," he said.

"Well, no, it's up to you actually. You said before he wouldn't ever think you'd go out with a guy with tattoos, so I can leave them down. It's no problem."

His eyes met mine, and he shook his head. "Up. Don't be someone you're not."

I scoffed out a laugh, though it was hardly funny. "Well, that's exactly what I am. Actually, that's what I get paid to be."

He looked away, like the individual threads on his clothes were the most fascinating things ever. "Yeah, I guess."

"But thank you," I said. "For wanting me to be me." He

had no idea what those simple words could possibly mean to someone like me.

He gave me a tight smile, then he pulled his sweater off by the hem and hung it back up straight away. Then he undid his shirt, and without a word, he slipped it off. He raked through his clothes, not finding what he wanted, then he went for his folded shirts. He plucked out a grey one, but before he could put it on, I said, "Stop."

He spun to look at me. "What?"

There I was, without one lick of shame, staring at his body. His very perfectly toned, perfectly defined chest and abs. "Fuck, Andrew."

"Oh," he said, and I almost groaned when his blush crept down his neck and over his chest. He fumbled with his shirt.

"Feel free not to wear that," I offered. "Because, Jesus."

"I told you I work out," he said, pulling the shirt on regardless of my almost begging him not to.

"Yeah, but you didn't say you were fucking hot."

He totally laughed me off, disregarding every compliment I could give him. Andrew was such a mixed bag. He was shy and a little meek even, yet so forthright in other ways. I could usually pick a top or bottom, but he left me utterly confused.

"Okay, personal question time," I announced.

He hung his head. "Oh, no."

His reaction made me smile. "Remember, you can veto me at any time."

"Sounds ominous," he mumbled but looked at me expectantly. Waiting, dreading...

"Eli. Did you top him, or did he top you?" I really had no business knowing. Sure, it told me the relationship dynamics between them, but I'd never asked any other of my clients anything so personal. But with Andrew, I needed to know. I wanted to know what he was like in bed.

He was shocked at first—that much was clear—and his clothes were suddenly fascinating again. His brows furrowed for a moment, and I thought he wasn't going to answer. But then he shrugged. "Both. Though it was…"

Both. God, he just kept on getting better. "Though it was, what?"

"Infrequent."

Infrequent? What the fucking hell was wrong with this Eli? Something definitely didn't add up with him. "I have serious concerns about Eli's state of mind."

He ignored my comment but stared right into my eyes. "Personal question," he repeated. He took my hand and inspected the tattoos on my arm, more specifically, he traced his finger along the biggest of the four blackbirds, and my heart just about stopped. *I wasn't ready for this kind of personal.* "What do these mean?"

I swallowed down the lump in my throat, not sure what to answer. Not sure I could. My tattoos, like most people's, were reminders, badges of personal experiences. Yes, I might wear them on my skin for the world to see, but their meaning was a little too personal. In the end, I shook my head. My voice was just a whisper. "Veto."

SIX

The bar had quite a crowd for a Sunday evening.

Andrew had been a little quiet since our conversation in his closet. The irony of that certainly wasn't lost on me. Thankfully he didn't push it, but he smiled kindly and tried a little too hard to make me feel better, almost like how someone treats a dog that's been kicked too much.

The irony of that wasn't lost on me either.

"Drink?" he asked. I nodded, and he went to the bar while I found us a table. He came back with two beers and handed me one. "Out of all the things I've asked, what drink you prefer was not one of them."

"It's perfect," I said. "You chose well."

The bar filled, getting busier and louder. We talked about random stuff. What places we've been, what we wanted to be when we were growing up, our most embarrassing moment ever, subjects at school we loved, those we hated, first crushes, first kisses. After three beers I almost forgot what we were there for. Until Andrew looked over my shoulder, his eyes widened and he paled.

I moved closer and put my hand on his waist. "Is Eli

here?" I asked quietly into his ear. I felt him nod rather than saw it. "Has he seen us?"

I could feel Andrew's chest rise and fall against mine, then he nodded. "Yeah. Just now."

"Good," I said, pulling back and giving him a smile. "This is what we wanted."

He looked at me with eyes I couldn't read. Scared? Unsure? Sorry?

Still with my hand on him, I leaned in again and whispered in his ear. "I want to know how far that blush creeps down your body."

He barked out a laugh, and as I'd presumed, he blushed. Which was the very reason I said it. "Jesus," he mumbled, sipping his beer.

I was grinning at him. It was the perfect reaction. If not for the dickhead ex-boyfriend, then it was for me. I didn't realise I had a thing for men who blushed.

I didn't realise I was starting to have a thing for Andrew.

Sure, I treated him differently to any other client I'd had, but that was just because we got on so well. Or so I told myself. It wasn't until there was a guy behind me who I'd still never laid eyes on that it really hit me...

I had feelings for Andrew.

I didn't know what I wanted. But I was pretty sure I didn't want Andrew to reconcile with Eli. Actually, I didn't even want him to speak to him.

I was failing at my job. Well, that wasn't exactly true. I was swaying my job for personal gain, and that was worse.

"What do I do?" he asked.

I was going to tell him to make his way to the bar. Give Eli the opportunity to make contact. But then Andrew put his hand on my chest, and that touch, that warmth changed everything.

"We bide our time," I whispered in his ear. I could smell his cologne, I could feel his body heat against me. It was heady, and I could barely speak. "We make him jealous. We make him realise what he walked away from."

Andrew's voice was breathy and hot in my ear. "He's watching."

God, my head was spinning, my heart was pounding. "Good," I murmured. And it *was* good. I wanted Eli to watch. I wanted to put my hand around Andrew's neck and kiss him. Fuck, I wanted to kiss him until he forgot his own name. I wanted to do more than that. I wasn't exactly lying about wanting to see how far that blush went down his body.

"Do we go or do we stay?" he whispered against the shell of my ear.

I didn't know. It was the first time since I'd started this gig that I had no clue what I was doing. I knew we should stay, I knew I should instigate a point of contact for my client, but I wasn't ready for this to be over.

Jesus, my head was all over the place. And not exactly ruled by reason. I wasn't thinking straight—if that wasn't the crux of all gay men's jokes—it wasn't just my dick that was making this decision. My stupid heart had a fair bit to say about it. Unfortunately, my even stupider brain wasn't anywhere to be found. "Let's get out of here."

I took his hand and led him through the bar, and that was when I spotted Eli. He was just like the photos I'd seen, and there was no doubt that he noticed I was wearing the vest he'd given Andrew because his eyes narrowed when he saw me in it, and there was no doubt he was watching Andrew.

I was trying not to smile when we got outside, but it was Andrew who laughed. "Did you see his face?"

"I did." I opened the door of the closest cab and held it for him. He slid into the back seat, and I joined him.

"What do we do now?" he asked. I wasn't sure if his excitement was because contact had been made or because we pulled off the illusion of being on a date or if it was the three beers he'd had, but his smile was beautiful.

I gave the cabbie Andrew's address. "We go back to your house and post some pics on Facebook."

He laughed again. His whole face was lit up, like he was some teenaged kid who just door-knocked and ran. It was kind of adorable. "You weren't joking when you said we'd get a reaction from him."

I agreed. "He looked shocked"

"I don't think he liked my vest on you."

"That was why I wore it."

He breathed out a quiet laugh, and I was waiting for realisation to kick in. The high of success was usually followed by a what-have-I-done? low, but with Andrew it never really came.

"Should I be concerned about what type of photos you want to put on my Facebook?" he asked as we walked into his living room.

"No. I said Facebook, not Grindr."

He laughed at that and walked through to the kitchen. I saw the still-not-connected record player and decided it needed to be working and was bent over the lowboy cabinet plugging the power cord in when Andrew came back in.

He was holding two beers and was totally checking my arse out. "Like what you see?" I asked with a raised eyebrow.

He held a bottle of beer out to me. "Shut up and drink it."

I took the beer with a laugh. "You were supposed to be the meek and polite guy. Not telling me to shut up and drink."

He took a swig of beer and smiled as he swallowed it. "Only in front of people I'm not comfortable with."

"Glad to hear that." I tapped my bottle to his. "Cheers."

There was a long few seconds where neither of us looked away, and it made my heart pound all out of rhythm and a warmth buzzed through my groin. If he weren't a client, I would have taken the bottle out of his hand, pushed him back on the sofa, and found every point of skin on his body that made him moan.

Completely oblivious to the pornographic images in my head, he fell back onto the sofa and put one foot up on the coffee table. "The LP won't play itself," he said.

I scoffed at him, picked up a cushion from the recliner, and threw it at him. "Bossy shit."

He caught the cushion easily and let it fall onto his lap. I wondered if it was to hide his arousal or if it was just me who was on edge. I knew without a doubt I'd be taking matters in to my own hands as soon as I got home.

I put the vinyl record onto the turntable and couldn't help but smile as that familiar crackle filled the room before Jeff Buckley started to play. Then, still facing the record player, I pointed to my arse. "You get a good look?"

I turned around, but he was looking at his phone. "Sorry, what was that?" he asked, still distracted.

"Nothing," I said. I sat down right beside him. "Did he message you?"

"Nope."

"He will."

"You sound pretty sure."

"Well, I'm good at what I do."

He blinked a few times and took a long pull of his beer, so I took his phone. I pressed the camera button and leaned back into the crook of his arm. I pulled his arm around my shoulder and totally manoeuvred us to look as close and casual as possible. I held the phone out to take a selfie of us, but the first picture looked wrong. He wasn't smiling.

"You're allowed to smile," I told him.

He did, but it was still too forced. So I dug my fingers into his ribs, and he jumped and laughed, almost spilling his beer. "Hey!" he cried, giving me a playful shove.

I kept my finger on the button as I turned my head, trying to bite his chest. He snorted out a laugh so I tickled him some more and we kind of reclined, with my back against his chest. His arm came back over my shoulder, his hand on my chest, holding me there. It was very relaxed, very natural. I held the phone up and snapped some more, and the photos showed a better smile on his face now. A more content smile.

"Perfect," I said. I pressed the Facebook app button, and seeing he had some notifications and messages—which were none of my business—I handed him back his phone. "Did you want to check those?"

He reached over to put his beer on the side table and took the phone. He could have easily used the hand that was resting on my chest, but he obviously liked where it was. I didn't exactly object.

"Mmm," he said. "Usual crap." He handed his phone back to me without a hint of hesitation.

I hit the upload picture button and selected the best one. It only showed half his face and the top of my head to my eyes, and it was kind of blurry, but it was clear we were both laughing. It was also pretty clear I had my head on his chest and his arm was around my shoulder. "This one?" I asked.

He looked at it for a second and answered with a nod.

"What do we say?" I asked.

"I don't know," he replied. "This is your domain."

I snorted and typed in *Best night ever*, and before I could question if it was too much, I hit Post. "Done."

He was silent, though I could feel his heart beating against the side of my head. But he never moved his arm from around me, and I still didn't object. It was literally only seconds later before the first *Likes* came through, followed by a few *LOLs* and two *Andrew????*s and one *Hey Andrew, I think someone stole your phone.*

Andrew huffed out a laugh. "That's Michelle. I work with her." Then his private messages dinged. "Aaaaand that's Sarah," he said with a sigh. He didn't read the messages though, and after about twenty seconds, his phone rang. His sister's name flashed on screen, and with a groan, he answered. "Hey."

I could really only hear the buzz of her voice, not the exact words, but it sounded like she said, "He's there with you now?"

"Well, yeah. Can we have this conversation tomorrow?"

I took a mouthful of beer and threaded the fingers of my free hand through his hand that was still around my shoulder. It was ridiculous how natural this was, how intimate and totally amazing it was. I hadn't had this kind of closeness in a long time. Sure, I'd had one-nighters, the occasional two-nighter, but nothing like this. Nothing like lazing on the sofa all snuggled in for a Sunday night.

"It was just to get a reaction from him, that's all," Andrew said. "No big deal."

No big deal.

Only it was. To me, at least. And there I was thinking I could get used to being like this with Andrew, before I remembered he was actually still in love with someone else. And that drove home a reality check like a Mack fucking truck.

The reality was, as nice as playing pretend boyfriends was, I still had a job to do. As much as I didn't want to do it. He was paying me to get his ex back.

Fucking Goddammit. I let go of his hand and sat up straight and faced him. "Can I speak to her?" I asked quietly.

He frowned. "Spencer wants to talk to you," he told her. After his sister said something I couldn't hear, he handed me the phone.

"Hi Sarah, it's Spencer," I said.

"Hi," she said, obviously unsure. "Nice photo."

"Oh, thanks."

"He talks about you," she said.

Oh.

Remember your job, Spencer. Remember what he's spending time with you for.

I cleared my throat. "Can I ask a favour?"

She was quiet, waiting for me to continue.

"Can you please comment on that photo about meeting us out next Saturday night?" I asked. "Say, 'Nine o'clock at Jazz and Blues Bar.'"

"Um, sure," she hedged. "Why?"

"So Eli will see it. You don't actually have to meet us at the bar, if you don't want. But we'll be there." I looked right at Andrew when I said, "And I can guarantee Eli will be too."

He held my gaze for a while before he picked up his beer and took a long drink.

"Spencer?" Sarah's voice in my ear startled me. "Can I ask you something?"

"Sure."

"How's Andrew been?"

"Fine," I replied. "Though it's not like I'd really know, is it?"

There was a long pause, then she said, "Hmm, I guess."

"Anyway," I said changing the subject completely, "he's looking at me funny. Though he did want me to tell you that he would love to cook dinner for you tomorrow night."

"No I didn't," he yelled with a shove to my arm.

I laughed and handed him the phone, with which he promptly told his sister he wasn't cooking her anything. Then he groaned and rolled his eyes. "Fine." After a few more grunts at her, he disconnected the call and shoved my arm again. "Now I have to freakin' cook dinner for her."

I burst out laughing. "You're welcome."

"She said you have to help me."

"She did not."

"She did so," he said, then drained his beer. "Be here at six."

I gaped. Seriously. Like a fish. "Really?"

He nodded. "Sharp. I don't care much for tardiness."

"I don't care much about the word tardiness, I have to say. I care even less about cooking."

He snorted. "My mother has probably just contacted the NSA to see where she can buy facial recognition software to try and figure out who the hell is in that photo with me, so you can put up with things like cooking and the word tardiness."

"You really are bossy."

One of his eyebrows flicked in a daring kind of way. Even a little suggestive, in a "wanna find out how bossy I can be?" kind of way. My dick nodded eagerly. And on that note, I knew I had to leave or I'd be doing something I'd regret. Well, okay, I wouldn't regret it. I'd enjoy every second of having my way with him, but it wouldn't be a very wise professional move. I stood up. "Right then," I said. "I better be going." I tried really hard to ignore the aching need to palm my half-hard dick, and it didn't help that he stared at my crotch.

Then his gaze raked up my body, like hot and teasing fingers. I swear I could feel it. When his eyes met mine, they were dark, and he looked like he wanted to devour me. I wasn't imagining it. I knew lust when I saw it. And I was pretty damn sure if I didn't turn and walk away right that second, I would have let him. I had to mentally tell my stupid feet to move. Not one part of me wanted to, but I did it. I somehow got to his front door.

"Let me call you a cab." I didn't realise he was right behind me.

Startled, I pulled the door open. "Nah, it's fine. I'll bus it. It's straight down the boulevard from here."

"Are you sure?"

No. But if I had to wait even five minutes for a cab to arrive, we wouldn't be needing the cab at all. I'd have him right there on the foyer floor. I swallowed hard. "Yep. I'm sure."

Ignoring how close he was, how good he smelled, how my body yearned to just touch him, I left.

Not even the funky smell of the bus or the weirdos on it were metaphorical cold water on how turned on I was. The lights in the tattoo shop were still on, but ignoring them as well, I went straight around the back and upstairs.

I threw my wallet and keys on the table and let out an embarrassingly loud groan when I palmed my dick. I was completely hard now, my dick straining against my hip, confined tight in my jeans. I toed out of my shoes and undid my fly as I walked into my bathroom, slid my jeans and briefs down, and freed my cock. I wrapped my hand around the shaft and gave myself a few long pulls.

Jesus, it felt so good.

I pulled my shirt—his shirt, whatever—off by the hem, taking the vest with it. I couldn't get out of my jeans quick enough and pulled my socks off with them. I turned the water on in the shower, thanking the hot water gods I didn't have to wait long. It really was so much less-messy to jerk off in the shower.

I rested my left forearm against the tiles and leaned my forehead against my arm. I'd been so turned on most of the day, this wasn't going to take long at all. All I could think about was Andrew. That look in his eyes when he saw the bulge in my jeans... God, I could imagine those eyes looking up at me while my dick was down his throat.

Fuck.

I'd bet any amount of money I hadn't been gone a minute before he had his hand around his own dick. I wondered how he pleasured himself, how he liked it. I pictured him with his head thrown back as he came. I imagined the sounds he'd make, I imagined what it would feel like for him to shoot down my throat, or in my arse.

And I came.

I couldn't even care about how quick it took. I didn't care the second time either, when I was in bed and jerked off to fantasies of me fucking him.

What I did care about was the flutter of hope in my chest. I tried to douse it with reality, but it was still fluttering when I fell asleep.

⁂

"AND YOU SAW THE EX?" Lola asked. It was lunchtime on Monday, and like always, we were hanging out in Emilio's tattoo shop.

"Yep."

"Did he initiate contact?"

"Nope. Not yet. We definitely had his attention though."

"When's the next point of contact?"

"I'm having dinner at his house tonight."

"With Andrew?"

"Well, not with Eli, that's for sure."

"You're not going out?" she asked. "Somewhere fancy? He seems like a fancy kind of guy."

"Well, no. I mean, he is, but it's just dinner. I have to help him cook," I admitted. "His sister lined it up, so unless she's bringing Eli with her, there's no chance of him seeing us." Lola was looking at me funny. Actually, so was Daniela. Even Emilio was smiling to himself. "What?"

"That doesn't sound like a job, Spence," Lola said. "That sounds like a date."

I scoffed. "He's a client!"

"Ever had dinner at any other client's place, on a Monday night?"

"Well, no," I answered. "But it's different. I dunno. It doesn't matter anyway. We've set the rendezvous point with the ex for the weekend. This time next week, it'll be all over."

Lola wasn't looking at me exactly. She was *watching* me. For what, I couldn't even guess. "And how do you think it will go?"

I shrugged. "I don't know. Something about the boyfriend is off. I can't put my finger on it—I have no clue, to be honest. He seems like a decent guy, but I think Andrew's better off without him."

"Mm mm," Lola said with a patronizing nod.

I knew what she was implying. I made a mental note to work on my game face, and instead of trying to deny it, I flipped her the bird. "Shut up."

She laughed and sipped her coffee. "Anyway, what I was going to call you about but decided you could buy me coffee instead was I need some help tomorrow and Wednesday. I have a two-day photoshoot."

Lola quite often did make-up for photoshoots and needed

me to help her carry all her stuff. "Sure. As long as you quit trying to imply anything about me and Andrew."

She smiled. "I can't promise that."

I rolled my eyes. "What time?"

"I'll pick you up at seven."

I STOOD on Andrew's front step right on six o'clock. I knocked and waited but there was no answer. My phone buzzed, and it was a message from him.

> Running late. Will be five minutes. Sorry.

I smiled as I replied.

> Tardiness is so unbecoming of you. Thought you didn't much care for it.

Not ten seconds later my phone rang. It was Andrew. "I'm driving and shouldn't have texted you. I should have called first. Are you pissed off? I said I was sorry."

He sounded genuinely worried. "What? No. I was just taking the piss."

"Oh."

"You're not driving while talking on the phone are you?" I asked. "That's just as dangerous as texting."

"I have you on Bluetooth."

"Oh. Is someone else in the car with you?"

"No, why?"

"Shame really. I was just going to say something sexually inappropriate to embarrass you, that's all."

He surprised me by laughing. "Sorry to disappoint you."

"I'll survive." I took a breath and realised I was smiling. "I think your neighbour thinks I'm a creeper."

"Why?"

"She gave me daggers as she walked inside. She pulled the door shut behind her really quickly like I was going to try and get in. I smiled at her and said I was waiting for you, but she very cheerfully told me she had mace in her handbag."

"Jesus."

I laughed. "I was afraid I'd have to break out some kung fu."

"Do you know kung fu?"

"No. That's why I was afraid."

He laughed at that. "Sounds like Constance. She lives directly above me. I can speak to her."

"No it's fine. She's a single girl living in LA. She *should* be suspicious of strange men hanging around the communal entrance to her apartment, ready to inflict excruciating pain at the first sign of creepiness."

He huffed out a laugh. "You didn't charm her?"

"I tried. My dashing smile and Aussie accent must only work on guys."

"Maybe it's the beard."

I gasped, feigning complete offense. "The horror! I love my beard," I said, as I automatically rubbed my whiskers.

"It suits you."

"Do you know how long it takes to get it just right?" I asked. "There is a small window of opportunity for perfection. Three days, max. The line between too short and too long is thin, my friend. I'm telling you. You don't know how easy you have it to be clean-shaven. Though I don't think a beard would suit you. Maybe some scruff on weekends."

"Just weekends?"

"Yeah, I figured you wouldn't want facial hair at work," I told him. "But I'm totally down with scruff on weekends."

"Is that right?" he asked. I was pretty sure he was smiling. It sounded like he'd stopped driving? Was that a car door?

"Hey, did you stop somewhere?"

"Maybe."

"Maybe? You either did or you didn't. Let me guess, you're at the store buying some fancy stuff I'm not gonna be able to cook, and your sister's gonna go all Gordon Ramsey on me."

He was quiet on the other end of the phone, and as I turned around I saw he was standing on the sidewalk, watching me. He had his phone to his ear, a stupid smile on his face, and he was holding a bag of takeout.

Still speaking into the phone, even though he could hear me just fine, I said, "You totally cheated."

He clicked off the call. "I did," he said, walking up to me. He handed me the bag of takeout, which was still hot, and put his key into the door. "I don't cook."

"Not at all?"

"If I can avoid it."

"Fair enough," I said, following him inside. He looked good, great actually. He had on grey pants, a light blue button-down shirt, sleeves rolled to his elbows, and a plain black knitted vest. I completely got caught staring at his arse.

He never called me on it, but he smiled when he took the bag. "Italian okay?"

"Perfect."

He loaded the takeout into the oven and set it to warm, then went about getting plates and stuff from cabinets. "I was going to order Vietnamese," he said. "There's a great little restaurant not far from here that does an amazing chicken and mango dish, amongst other things. Anyway, I called ahead and told them I'd need an ingredient list so I could order and explained the shellfish allergy. She kept trying to tell me I meant menu, and I had to keep saying 'no, full ingredient list, including the ingredients of any sauces.' Anyway, after twenty minutes of this, she refused. Starting yelling at me in Vietnamese. So I told her I didn't care how good her *Goi Ga* is, she could shove it."

I couldn't believe it. "You didn't?"

"I did," he answered. Then stopped what he was doing and stared at me. "Why? Shouldn't I have done that?"

I let out a laugh. "No, that's fine by me. It's just that, well, no one has done that for me before."

"How could they not have?" he asked. Apparently it was a rhetorical question because he didn't give me time to answer. "I'd rather you didn't drop dead of anaphylaxis on my living room floor, thanks."

I chuckled at that. "Yeah, I'd rather I didn't either."

He handed me a pile of placemats and waved his hand at the plates and serving utensils, like I'd won them on a game show. "Tonight's lucky contestant gets to set the table while I go upstairs and get changed."

I was still chuckling to myself when he walked back into the room. He was wearing jeans and a T-shirt. It was the most casual I'd ever seen him, and he still managed to look hot. I liked his geeky sweaters on him, but they hid his body. And seriously, he had a fucking great body.

"Is this okay?" he looked down at himself. "I just thought..."

And there he was again with the self-doubt. "You look great. I was just admiring the view, that's all."

He shook his head at me, like the notion was ridiculous. Ignoring me altogether, he went into the kitchen and came back out with a bottle of wine and three glasses. "Do you drink merlot?"

"Sure," I answered, taking the glasses from him and putting them on the table. "What time will Sarah be here?"

Right then, there was a knock at the door.

Andrew shrugged. "Oh, any minute now."

I laughed and was still smiling as Andrew opened the door. As they both came back in, I was struck by how much they actually looked alike. There was definitely a silent, eyeballing conversation going on between them. It was like she was hinting at something and he was telling her to shut up.

"Spencer," she greeted me warmly. "Nice to see you again."

"Likewise," I replied. And for some unknown reason, I was nervous. I normally had the knack to work any room, regardless of my comfort level. But this was different, and Lola's words of "sounds more like a date to me" skidded into my head. I wiped my hands down my thighs and struggled to find what to say next.

Thankfully Andrew spoke first. "So Spencer was just trying to convince me to tell you he cooked dinner and that I didn't get takeout."

My mouth fell open. "I did not!" Andrew laughed as he walked past me and into the kitchen. I pushed his shoulder. "Liar."

Sarah laughed and said, "Don't worry, Spencer, I know anything that comes out of this kitchen isn't homemade."

"So, he's a notorious non-cooker?"

"Oh yes," she said, nodding her head. "It's not that he *won't* cook. It's that he *can't* cook. I'm pretty sure he could burn water."

"I can hear you, you know?" he called out. "Now, come in here and help me."

"Is he always so bossy?" I asked Sarah.

She rolled her eyes. "Always."

"Yep. Still hearing you," he said, and I grinned as I walked into the kitchen. He had taken the dishes from the oven and put them on the counter. He threw a dishtowel at me. "They're hot, so be careful."

I snorted out a laugh. "Is that how you ask someone to take food to the table?"

"Well, it's the least you could do, considering how many hours I slaved away in here," he said without missing a beat.

I chuckled as I carried the takeout containers to the table. Sarah was looking at us with the same twisted-lip pout that Lola got when she was trying not to smile, and then they were having that silent eyeball conversation again, which I pretended not to notice.

And that's pretty much how dinner went. Comfortable, funny, never-ending conversation. I liked Sarah. She was smart and cultured, like her brother. They talked of everything from world issues to reality television. And something I found really peculiar was not once did Eli's name come up.

I don't know why, but I'd expected him to be a large part of our conversation topic. He was, after all, the reason the three of us were together. But nope. Not once. Not that I minded. I'd rather not talk about him at all. I had a hard enough time wondering when Andrew missed him the most... Did he lay in bed and wish he was there? Did he miss the sound of him coming down the stairs in the morning? Did he miss putting his arms around him? Did he miss him at all? Because the more I got to know Andrew, I had to wonder where Eli fit in.

Normally when I took on a job, there was a gaping hole in my clients' lives where their partners used to be, that void they were trying to fill. But Andrew seemed so complete. He was a confounding man that much was for certain.

"Spencer?"

Shit. Andrew must have asked me something. "Huh? Sorry, I was a million miles away."

Andrew looked at me quizzically. "Sarah wanted to know about the record player. I told her to ask the guy who bought it for me."

Oh. "Oh, sure. Want me to play the album as well?" I asked. Glad for the distraction, I stood up and put the record onto the turntable and lowered the tonearm, and soon Jeff Buckley was singing to the three of us. I sat back down and took a sip of my wine, with no clue of the conversation I'd missed.

Sarah tilted her head, listening to the music. "It's lovely."

Andrew put his glass down on the table and excused himself, I presumed, to go to the bathroom. He shot a well-aimed *be nice* glare at his sister, and then it was just me and Sarah. I knew she was going to ask me questions, and I didn't have to wait long.

"So," she started. "I have to say, I'm surprised you bought him a record player."

She didn't ask it as a question, but it totally was. What she was really asking was *Why did you buy him a record player? Do you buy all your clients record players?* I gave her a smile and sipped my wine. "I'm surprised he didn't have one."

"You've been spending a bit of time with him," she said, totally asking in a non-question kind of way.

"I have. He's a nice guy."

"Just nice?"

I cleared my throat and steered the conversation. "Tell me about Eli?"

She sat back in her seat and took her wine glass off the table. "Eli's a... nice guy."

"But?"

"But he wasn't right for him." She frowned at her own words. "I don't know. They just didn't seem to fit. It was so odd. They had nothing in common, and when Andrew told me they were talking about getting married," she leaned in and whispered, "I almost freakin' died."

"Whose idea was it to hire me?"

"Mine," she said. "I just want him happy. And if Eli makes him happy, then that's what I want."

"Did Eli make him happy?"

Before she could answer, Andrew came back. He looked between us warily, knowing full well he was the subject of our conversation. "Everything okay?"

"Yep," Sarah answered. "Spencer and I were just arguing over who was going to clean up. He lost, so he has to do it."

A bubble of laughter escaped me. "I totally didn't, but I will clean up." I put the empty takeout trays on top of one another and started to stack plates. "I could just imagine you two as kids."

Andrew took the plate from me. "You don't have to clean up anything," he said. "And our childhood was quite normal. Well, after Sarah realised she'd never win an argument with me, we got along just fine."

"So, tell us about your childhood," Sarah asked. "What was life like growing up in Australia?"

There was a dull thud, and I was pretty sure it was Andrew kicking his sister under the table. He was cautious of asking questions of my family, no doubt reading into the veto I gave him the other day. "My childhood was fine," I said, looking at him. I'm pretty sure he heard the unsaid teenage years weren't so great. "I had a pretty good childhood actually. I grew up in Sydney, and we rode our bikes down to the soccer fields, to the corner shop, that kind of thing."

Sarah very astutely, and somewhat obviously, changed the subject. "So do you get asked about your accent all the time?"

I nodded. "All the time. And can I just say, asking me to say throw a shrimp on the barbie is not conducive to keeping one's teeth."

They both laughed. "People have asked you to say that?" Andrew asked.

"You'd be surprised. Though my friends are used to it now, but at first they'd crack up at some of the things I'd say."

Andrew was smiling. "Like?"

So I told them funny stories, using words like *servo* and *arvo*, *sunnies* and *chooks*, and the differences between mate and maaaaaaate. And all the while Sarah sat back and watched us. Well, mostly she watched Andrew. And not long after, she looked at her watch and stood up. "I didn't realise it was so late," she said.

"It's not even nine," Andrew countered.

"Yes well," she said, grabbing her coat and handbag. "I better be going. I'll leave you guys to clean up."

"Yeah, thanks," Andrew mumbled. Throwing his napkin onto the table, he stood, as did I.

She kissed her brother's cheek. "I'll call you tomorrow." Then she looked at me. "The answer to your question is no. I thought so, but no. Spencer, it was really nice to see you again." And with a smile, she was gone.

Huh. Weird.

"What did she mean?" Andrew asked, staring at the door Sarah had just gone out of. "Answer to what question?"

"Um." I sat back down and tried to recall what I'd asked her. "I can't remember."

We were talking about Eli... Oh. That's right. *Did Eli make him happy?*

Her answer: I thought so, but no.

"Um, it was about the record player," I lied. "I asked her if she wanted me to get her one."

The way Andrew looked at me, I knew he knew I was lying. God, I was struggling to keep up the façade with him. Normally untruths just rolled off my tongue. I'd spent most of my teenage years lying about who I was, then now as a dial-a-boyfriend, it was what I did for a living.

"You can't lie for shit," he said, picking up the stack of plates.

"Shush," I said, just as Jeff Buckley started to sing "Hallelujah." I breathed in deep, as though I could inhale the music. "It's my favourite song."

He made a face at me, though stopped short at sticking his tongue out before he picked up the dirty plates. I helped him pack them all into his dishwasher and tidy up, and in no time at all, everything was back to perfect. "So what time do you start with Lola tomorrow?" he asked when we were done in the kitchen. I'd told him how I sometimes help her out when she needs me, mostly carrying her boxes and bags, or just being an extra pair of hands. It was never strictly exciting work, but I loved spending time with Lola.

"Seven, so I probably should get going soon." I didn't really want to leave but couldn't think of any reason to stay. Well, any reason for him to want me to stay. I took the record off the turntable and slipped it back into its cover. Then I realised his piano was just sitting there, all neglected and unplayed, and I really wanted to hear what he could do. "Would you play me something on your piano?"

His eyes shot to mine, wide and shocked, as though I'd just asked him to have sex with me. "Um…"

"You don't have to," I said, giving him an out.

"Are you sure?"

I scoffed. "Of course I'm sure." Actually, there wasn't

much else I was sure about. But hearing him play the piano was a definite yes.

"What will I play?"

"First thing you think of."

He blinked a couple of times, still so unsure, and walked over to the piano. He sat down slowly and put his fingers to the keys. And without another word, he took a deep breath and started to play.

Such a sweet song, with patient, perfectly timed finesse. I'd never heard anything like it.

I didn't know what the song was called, who wrote it, composed it, nothing. But it stole my breath. It wasn't just the music. It was the man who made angels sing from his piano. *He* stole my breath, how his hands moved, how he closed his eyes and got lost in the music, how he coerced the sounds from the piano with his whole body. And when his hands fell to his lap and the last note hung in the air, I couldn't find the words.

Andrew glanced at me, before he looked back at the piano and he exhaled through puffed out cheeks.

I swallowed down the emotions, the butterflies that swarmed my chest. He was waiting for me to respond, so I told him the God's honest truth. The best I could manage was a whisper. "I've never seen anything so beautiful."

He gave me a coy, embarrassed smile. "Don't you mean *heard*?"

"Isn't that what I said?" I asked, confused. My heart was still pounding, an erratic metronome. *I was sure I said heard.*

Andrew shook his head and smiled down at his hands. "Better than 'Hallelujah' by Jeff Buckley?"

I laughed off my embarrassment at my own reaction to him. "Andrew, that was incredible. What song was it?"

"Just something I wrote."

I scoffed. "Are you kidding me? You wrote that?"

He nodded.

"Just something I wrote." I mimicked his voice. "No, a grocery list is just something you write, that—*that*"—I waved my hand at his piano,—"was, my God, Andrew, that was so... incredible." There just wasn't another word for it.

The smile he gave me was pure relief and maybe a dash of pride. "Thank you."

I had to stop myself from walking over and touching him. From putting my hands to his face and kissing him. From taking his hand and leading him upstairs to bed. I wanted to. Fuck, how I wanted to.

And I knew then that I was in over my head.

Somewhere, somehow, I'd let myself cross the line. And I hadn't just merely stepped over it. Oh no. I'd crossed that line like Usain freakin' Bolt. And instead of putting a stop to it, instead of stepping back and doing my actual job, my stupid heart went and spoke before my stupid brain.

"Play it again."

SEVEN

Lola pulled up out front of the shop and I jumped into the passenger side before the car behind her could honk. She drove her little 80s model Honda hatch—aptly named Cindy Crawford, after Lola's favourite 80s model—like a demon through morning traffic. And to her credit, she made it two whole blocks before she started with the questions. "So, how was dinner?"

"Good.

She glanced from the road to me. "Just good?"

I tried not to smile and failed. "Okay, so it was better than good. Lola, he played his piano for me last night."

"Is that a euphemism for something dirty?"

I laughed at that. "No. He actually played his piano. It was incredible."

"Was Sarah still there?"

"No. Just me."

"Oh, really?"

"Shut up. It wasn't like that. I asked him to play something, and he did. I mean, he has a grand piano sitting in his living room, for God's sake. It's not like I bought him a piano so he could play."

"Like you bought him a record player?"

I gave her the best shut-up glare I could manage. "That was different."

"Mm mm," she made that assent noise that wasn't really agreeing at all.

"Everyone should have a record player and at least one Jeff Buckley album," I said. "I'm sure it's a written rule somewhere."

She laughed. "What did he play you?"

"He said it was something he wrote. You know, like we write down a phone message, he writes music."

"Is there ànything he can't do?"

"Cook, apparently. He sucks at it."

Lola laughed. "Oh, good. For a second there I thought he was utterly perfect."

I rolled my eyes at her. "He orders good food though. It was a bunch of pastas and some veal dish."

She glanced at me a few times, like she was trying to figure out how to phrase something, and normally I'd tell her to just spit it out. But I was pretty sure I didn't want to hear whatever it was she was about to say if it involved Andrew, so I changed the subject. "So, where are we off to?"

"Downtown," she said. "It's a metro shoot."

"Cool."

And she didn't bring up Andrew again for the rest of the day. Granted, she was busy transforming beautiful people into extraordinarily beautiful people, and I was busy doing what she asked me to do. But our topic of conversation revolved around other things, and that was fine with me. That was until we finally climbed into Cindy Crawford and headed home, and I checked my phone. She drove like a crazy blind woman so sometimes it was best not to look up anyway.

"Checking for messages from anyone in particular?" she asked.

"I sent him a message earlier," I answered. "Just seeing if he replied."

Which he hadn't.

"Lining up another dinner date?"

"It's not like that."

"Mm mm." Again with the sarcastic course-not sound.

"I asked him if Eli had contacted him," I admitted. "We uploaded a photo onto his Facebook, and his sister commented with a time and place we'd be meeting this Saturday. I just wondered whether Eli had taken the bait, that's all."

"It's okay, Spence," she said. "You don't need to justify anything to me."

"I know. I'm not," I said. But I totally was, and we both knew it. I wanted to tell her I was struggling with this job. I wanted to tell her it was amazing and terrifying and horrible and wonderful. But I didn't. The cold reality was my job with Andrew would be over in five days. Come Sunday morning, we'd know whether Eli wanted him back. I mean the guy would have to be crazy if he didn't. "Can you watch the road and not me? I don't feel like dying today."

Lola scowled at me as my phone buzzed. It was Andrew, and the way my heart tripped over its own stupid feet was ridiculous.

Sorry, been a busy day. Just finished work and saw your message now. I had a message from Eli as well. What should I do?

And that stupid heart-tripping feeling became a lot more like heart-sinking. God I was so stupid.

> What did he say?

> Wanted to say hi. See how I was. Saw the photo, wanted to know if it was for real?

"What is it?" Lola asked. She looked from the traffic to me, her eyes etched with worry.

"Nothing," I lied. "It's Andrew. Said Eli's been in touch. He saw the photo."

"Is that good?" she asked slowly, clearly unsure.

I nodded. "Yep. It's what Andrew wants."

Lola had gone from unsure to concerned. "Spencer?"

"No, it's good. It's exactly why I suggested taking the photos and putting them on his Facebook," I answered, looking at my phone. Then I replied to Andrew's text, telling him to do the very thing I dreaded most.

> Message him back. Tell him you're not sure where things stand with me. Tell him it depends on how much time and space he needs. That should get a response.

With a deep breath, I turned my phone off. When I looked up, I realised we'd stopped across the road from the tattoo shop. Shit. I quickly undid my seatbelt and opened the door.

"Spencer," Lola started to say.

I got out and leaned down to speak through the door. "See you tomorrow at seven. I'll bring coffee," I said before I shut the door and tapped the roof of Cindy Crawford.

The car behind her honked his horn, and Lola flipped him the bird before taking off at warp speed into the flow of cars. I laughed and took my chances crossing the street in peak-hour traffic.

———

I CLIMBED BACK into Cindy Crawford right on seven Wednesday morning. I had a takeout tray with a coffee for Lola and a tea for me. I waited until we were moving through traffic and I felt safe enough before I handed it to her.

"You didn't answer my texts last night," she said.

"Sorry about that," I mumbled. "I had my phone off."

"Spencer, can we talk about it?"

I shook my head. "I'm fine. Please watch the road."

"Don't change the subject. You can't avoid shit like this forever."

"Yes, I can. I've done it for years. It works just fine."

"You're allowed to feel things, Spencer."

"I know that."

"Do you?"

"I thought we weren't talking about it," I said, looking out the window.

"One more question, then I'll leave it alone." She was gonna ask it whether I wanted her to or not, so there was no point in arguing. "Did Andrew reply?"

"I don't know. I turned my phone off."

"You haven't looked at all?"

Still looking out the window, I shook my head. She didn't say any more, but the sigh she let out may as well have been an "Oh, Spencer."

I helped her carry all her boxes and pull make-up bags on wheels down city streets until we reached the photoshoot. Lola and a few other make-up artists soon got busy doing their thing with the models, and I hung back out of the way.

Normally when I helped out at these things, I'd score a phone number and a one-night stand. But these pretty boys didn't interest me today, and by 10:00 a.m. my phone started to burn a hole in my pocket.

Well, wondering whether Andrew replied had started to burn a hole in my brain. Same thing really.

So I walked down the street a ways and turned on my phone. I had a bunch of missed calls and text messages. I checked the text messages first. Without reading them, I could see two from Lola, no doubt saying *Answer your goddamn phone*, two from Andrew, and one from a number I didn't recognise.

I opened the unknown number message first. It was a prospective new client named Lance, who got my number from my old client Gerrard, the super-rich arsehole guy, wondering if I was available to meet with him. I sighed. The idea of meeting another guy to go through the whole getting-to-know-you phase again seemed like torture. I considered hitting delete but didn't. It wasn't like I needed the money, but ordinarily I really liked my job. I figured I'd be back to normal next week so I was resigned to calling Lance later.

That left Andrew's texts. The first was sent not long after I replied telling him to reply to Eli.

> Okay. Message sent.

Then an hour after that was another.

> He called me. Wanted to know what I was doing on Saturday night. I told him I had plans, which he admitted to seeing on Facebook. Then he suggested Friday night. I told him I'd let him know. What do I do now?

Oh, fuck.

I took a deep breath in and let it out slowly. Then another. I didn't know if he'd called him back, if he'd agreed to meet him. God, he could have ended up calling back, and for all I knew, they'd reconciled and spent the night in bed.

I felt sick.

I stared at my phone screen, then I stared at it some more.

And with a sense of dread, I listened to the voice messages. There were two from Lola, saying exactly what I thought. The second wasn't as pleasant as the first, and I knew I'd have to apologise to her. The remaining three were from Andrew. The first was rather cheerful. "Hey, it's me. Um, Andrew. Andrew Landon." I smiled at that. "Eli called me. Can you give me a call back? Thanks."

Then the second voice message was forty minutes after the first, and he sounded a little anxious. "It's um, it's Andrew again. Not sure if you got my last message. I told Eli I'd let him know about Friday, but I wanted to talk to you first. I'm not sure what you want me to do."

The third voice message was two hours after that. His voice was quiet. "It's Andrew. I um... Call me."

The sound of his self-doubt expanded like a lead balloon in my chest. I hated that I caused him to doubt himself. Of all the people who should be confident. God, he was successful, talented, and sexy as hell. But he was also honest and funny, and for some reason he didn't see himself the way he should.

I guessed Eli leaving him would have hit his confidence hard, but it was like he'd been downtrodden or constantly told he wasn't quite good enough, and to think I'd added fuel to his fire of insecurity just about killed me.

I hit his number and put the phone to my ear. Given it was mid-morning and he'd be at work, I was expecting it to go to voicemail but was still disappointed when it did.

"Hey, it's me, Spencer. I'm really sorry I missed your calls and texts. I wasn't feeling well," I lied, "and had my phone off. I should have responded regardless, and I'm sorry I didn't."

He just had no idea how sorry I was.

"Just wondering if you called Eli back? Whether you're going out with him on Friday?" I cleared my throat. "Call me when you can. And again, Andrew, I'm sorry I let you down."

I clicked off the call and exhaled through puffed out cheeks. God, this was so fucked up. This feeling... this horrible feeling was a heavy, aching reminder of why I put up walls and kept my distance.

It was also a stark reminder that this was a professional transaction. He was paying me to get results, and I'd failed him. I should have taken his calls, and I should have told him, without any hesitation, to go out with Eli on Friday night.

Hell, maybe they did get back together last night. Maybe we wouldn't get a result on Saturday night because maybe we already had one, and maybe Andrew wasn't my client anymore. Maybe I needed to man the fuck up and get over it.

Wouldn't be the first time.

So, with that mindset, I opened the text from Lance, the prospective new client, and hit reply. *Sure. Does this Monday suit?*

I headed back up to the photoshoot to where Lola was working her magic on some over-tired, under-fed girl. As I walked in, one of the male models gave me a nod. "Hey," he said gruffly. He looked me up and down and gave me a smirk, which I'm sure on any other day would have worked for a phone number or a blowjob. But not today.

"Hey," I said, just to be polite, and kept walking. Lola didn't miss it, of course, and raised an eyebrow at me and a sad shake of her head. Ignoring whatever it was she was implying, I asked, "Need anything?"

"No," she said brightly, adding some black to the model's eyes with perfection. "Called Andrew yet?"

I thought about not answering but remembered her concerned messages on my phone. "I left a message."

"Good," she said with a fond smile. Like it was some huge personal milestone. I don't know, maybe it was.

I spent the rest of the day between doing whatever Lola told me to do and checking my phone. No reply from Andrew. I couldn't say I blamed him, after all, I'd ignored him. And by the time I'd loaded the last of Lola's equipment into Cindy Crawford, I had pretty much convinced myself that Andrew couldn't reply because he'd spent the day in bed with Eli.

No replies and a vivid imagination would do that.

"He'll call you," Lola said. She must have read my mind because I hadn't mentioned him for hours. "Don't look at me like that. It's written all over your face."

"It's stupid," I finally admitted. "I've known him for what? Not even two weeks."

"But you like him." It wasn't a question.

"He's a client," I said quietly, "who wants me to help him get back with his ex."

"Well, fate is a funny bitch," Lola said. "She has a way of making things right. Look at me and Gabe."

I nodded. They were perfect for each other. Life tried to split them up, but as it turned out, fate stepped in and righted that wrong. Well, fate *and* me, but mostly fate. "You're my best success story."

"And we owe it all to you."

Silence stretched out for a while which didn't happen often between us. It wasn't uncomfortable, it was just there. I was happy to wallow in self-misery anyway.

"You'll have your own success story," Lola said eventually. "Spencer, you deserve to be happy. There is someone out there, just for you. You'll see."

I huffed out a laugh. "Yeah right."

"And if Andrew decides he wants Eli instead, then it wasn't meant to be. And it'd be his loss. But you watch," she said, as she swerved lanes. "He'll call you."

And like she had ESP or something, my phone rang. Andrew's name flashed on the screen. My heart pounded and I smiled when I saw it was him, but then it occurred to me... "What if he's calling to tell me he and Eli are back together?"

Lola stared at me. "Answer the phone."

"Watch the road!"

She yelled, "Answer your damn phone!"

I pressed the answer button more out of panic than anything else. "Hey," I said, trying to sound as casual as I could.

"Are you okay?" he asked. No hello, no small talk. "You sounded terrible in your message. You said you didn't feel well? I've been in meetings all day, and I just got your message now."

"Nah, I'm okay. I feel a bit better now," I said. I risked a look at Lola and cringed when she was glaring at me for lying to him. "Sorry I missed your calls last night. How did it go with Eli?"

I almost didn't want to know. I almost told him to forget I asked, but he spoke first. "I um, I haven't answered him yet."

Oh. Oh, thank fucking God. "Oh," I said. I almost laughed with relief. Lola grinned and nodded at me. It was ridiculous.

"Well, I wasn't sure what you would want me to do," he said. "You're the expert in this, and I didn't want to do the wrong thing."

"No, you did the right thing," I told him, which wasn't

exactly the truth. "Making him wait for a day won't hurt him. In fact, it might make him realise a little sooner, yeah?"

"Hmm, maybe." He sounded unsure.

I exhaled loudly. The knot of unease in my chest had let up a little. I felt better than I had all day. In fact, my stupid brain had to actually tell my stupid mouth to stop smiling, and Lola giggled. "Shut up," I said, making her laugh.

Andrew's voice was quiet. "Sorry?"

"Oh, no not you!" I said quickly into the phone. "Lola's being a pain in my arse."

"Oh," he replied. "Should I call you later?"

"Actually, can I call you back in like ten minutes?" I asked. "I need my hands free for when Lola pulls up out the front of my place because she only slows down to thirty miles per hour and I have to commando-roll out of the car."

She whacked my arm, and Andrew laughed in my ear. "Okay. Good luck," he said. "And remember, keep your chin in and both arms up to protect your face. Avoid the kerb."

I laughed at his commando-roll tips, and he disconnected the call. Lola was grinning widely at me. I ignored her. "I'd really prefer you watch the road when you drive," I said, trying to act all cool about everything. "And I know what you're about to say about Andrew, and I'd also really prefer you didn't."

She did a little dance-butt wiggle in her seat. "I'm not saying anything you apparently don't already know."

"I'm pleading the fifth."

"You're Australian. You don't have the fifth."

I let out a laugh. My mood had done a complete one-eighty from this morning. And as much as I wanted to admit to Lola what I presumed she already knew—that Andrew was different to any other client I'd had—I wasn't ready to. It would make it real. And the truth was, at that very moment, Andrew was still my client. The objective was still open.

Thankfully, and somewhat death-defyingly, Lola weaved through two lanes and pulled up across from the tattoo shop like a race car driver. I jumped out and waved her off, and she was still smiling as she pulled Cindy Crawford back into traffic.

And with no clue what to tell Andrew about what to do about Eli, I pulled out my phone, found Andrew's number, and hit call. He answered on the first ring. "Hey, sorry about that. Evel Knievel just dropped me off before hurling Cindy Crawford at some poor law abiding road users."

Andrew snorted. "What?"

I waited for a break in the traffic before crossing the street. "Lola. She drives like a maniac."

"And what happened to Cindy Crawford?"

"Oh, that's her car. It's a cute little 80s model."

Andrew cracked up, and the warm sound of his laughter sent a flush of warmth through my chest. "Andrew, I'm really sorry I missed your calls last night."

"That's okay," he said. He sounded genuine. "You're better now though?"

"Yeah, much."

"Well, maybe I could come around?" he asked. "I just left work, so I'm already in the car. We could work out what to do about this Friday?"

"Sounds great."

"Okay. I'll park out back."

"Just come straight up to my door."

"See you in about twenty minutes." And he disconnected the call.

I pushed the door open to Emilio's shop and he looked up

from tattooing his customer. Then he looked at me again. "Jesus. The cat that got the canary."

I laughed him off. "Hey man. How's your day been?"

"Not as good as yours by the look of that smile."

I rolled my eyes. "Need anything?"

"Nah, I'm all good, my friend," Emilio said. "Oh, new magazines came in today. They're on the counter," he said, nodding toward the service desk.

"Cool." Emilio always subscribed to a few copies because customers tended to either dog-ear a page or just rip them out. I picked up the top copy. "I'll bring it back down later. You here late tonight?"

Emilio had his head down and was busy inking his customer. "Yeah man. Daniela's having the night off. Last client is at seven. It's just me."

"Want me to bring you some dinner or something?"

"Sweet, thanks."

I took the tattoo magazine and let myself out the back door and pulled it shut behind me. Upstairs, knowing Andrew wouldn't be far away, I freshened up. I washed my face, sprayed on some deodorant, and stopped myself from brushing my teeth. I mean, it was ridiculous. So I planted myself on the sofa and flicked through the magazine until there was a knock at the door.

When I opened the door, Andrew was standing there like a remedy for heart palpitations. Or maybe he made them worse. It was hard to tell. "Hey."

His smile was warm and wide. "Hey. You look good," he said. Then froze. "I mean, you look not-sick anymore."

I laughed, all relieved and nervous, and stepped aside, a silent invitation to come inside. "I'm much better." And that wasn't a lie. I *was* feeling much better. "Can I get you a drink or something?"

"Sure." He walked straight in, over to the sofa and sat down. He picked up the tattoo magazine and started thumbing through it. "Looking for new ideas?"

I handed him a bottled water and sat beside him. "Not really. I stole it from Emilio," I explained. "I just like to see what's new."

"They're pretty good," he said, tilting his head. "I'm surprised actually, by how much I like them."

"Would you ever get one?"

His eyes widened and he barked out a laugh. "Ah, no." Then he frowned. "Well, I've never thought about it."

"Not ever?"

He shook his head. "Nope." He took a mouthful of water and kept turning pages. He didn't look at me when he asked, "When did you get your first tattoo?"

"Sixteen. My Aunt Marvie took me to get it." My left hand automatically went to the top of my right arm. "The tribal cross was my first. It's been incorporated into the entire sleeve now, but yeah, that was my first tattoo."

His eyes shot to mine then. "Wow."

I shrugged, and he knew the ink on my arms, no matter how visible, was a private thing. "They're addictive."

"Would you get another one?" he asked. "Your sleeves are done, so where else would you get one?"

"Maybe a chest piece," I said, leaning back on the sofa. "I dunno."

"Colour or black and white?" he said, looking back to the magazine. "You have a mix of both on your arms."

"Depends on the piece," I said. "And what it means."

"Fair enough."

"How was work?"

He looked at me and smiled. "Good. How was your day with Lola?"

"Yeah, good. Busy. She's bossy."

Smiling, he kept looking at the pictures in the magazine. It was easy to forget he appreciated the tattoos from an artist's perspective, not a client's. "Oh," I said. "I need to get Emilio something to eat later on. Don't let me forget."

Andrew stayed until dinner. We got take out and ate it downstairs in the shop with Emilio after he closed for the day. Emilio and Andrew talked about lines and definition, shading and interpretation.

And not once did we talk about Eli.

EIGHT

Thursday afternoon I found myself on the street across the road from Eli's place of employment. A printing business I really had no need for going to, just a burning curiosity and a healthy dash of jealousy.

Well, maybe jealousy was a strong word, but I wanted to know what attracted Andrew to Eli. They met in a grocery store, which was the stuff of chick-flicks. A little too cliché? I wasn't sure. But Eli moved in with him. They had a history. An intimate history. Eli had touched Andrew in ways I wanted to but couldn't. Andrew had taken *him* to bed, kissed him, fucked him. And I wanted to see why.

Before I could talk myself out of it, I crossed the street and walked through the front door. A bell chimed to announce my entrance, and not a moment later, a woman came to the counter. I recognised Terri from the Facebook photo and then at the bar where she'd had birthday drinks and invited Eli to go with. Her name tag confirmed it. "Can I help you?" she asked brightly.

The foyer was kind of old but clean. There were product deals plastered on the walls. "Yeah. I'm just looking at the moment, but I have a business convention coming up I could need some marketing products for."

She went into a spiel of mail-outs, flyers, online ads, and I went along with it, nodding thoughtfully. She explained minimum numbers, maximums, payment options, and a whole lotta other crap I really wasn't interested in. "So, what's your target market?" she asked. "What kind of convention?"

I said the first thing that came to mind. "Tattoos," I answered, like that explained everything. "Could I have example art printed on canvas? Or framed even. I want an executive look, high-class. I want it to look like pieces from a photography studio."

Her eyes lit up. "Oh yes. Hang on, I'll just grab Eli. He's the man you want for that."

She disappeared and a sick nervous feeling twisted in my belly. He wasn't the man I wanted at all, but whether this was a good idea or a really fucking stupid idea, it was too late. Because Eli walked out from the staff-only door. Terri led the way. "This is Eli," she said. "He does all the prints like you're talking about." And she left us alone. Just me and him.

Eli was about my height, kind of handsome with his dark hair and dark eyes. He looked like a normal guy, just like the photos I'd seen. I hated him. Irrational, I know, but whatever. His eyes flickered with something when he saw me, and if he recognised me as the guy with Andrew from the bar the other night, he didn't say.

"Hi," he said, offering me his hand.

I shook it a little harder than normal, but whatever. If he was waiting for me to give him my name, I didn't.

"So, you're after framed prints?"

"I think so. I'm just getting prices at this stage." As much as I totally didn't care about wasting ten minutes of his time, I didn't want to waste the company's money thinking this was going anywhere. "How much time do you need, say for ten prints, sixty inches squared?"

He prattled on about prices and products, clearly trying to sell me a deal. Some would think he was good at his job. I, on the other hand, thought he was smarmy. I didn't care how good he was with the products he sold, he'd been with Andrew, and that made him a dick to me.

By some grace of God, my phone rang. It was Lola. I made a somewhat-apologetic face to Eli. "Sorry, I need to take this." I didn't wait for a reply from him, I just hit answer. "Hello."

"I'm at the shop. Where are you?"

I pretended to be disgruntled. I pressed my fingers into my eyes. "You're there now?"

"I just said that," she said. "Does spanking the monkey make you deaf?"

I choked on a laugh. "Right. Well, that's what he said."

It took her a second. It wasn't the first time I'd needed her to bail me out of a situation. She was pretty quick with these things now. "Oh. You're somewhere you shouldn't be, talking to someone you shouldn't be, aren't you?"

"That's correct."

"Does this have anything to do with Andrew?"

"Yes."

"You went and checked out the ex, didn't you?"

"Of course."

"Is he right in front of you?"

I sighed loudly. "Yes. Okay, I'll come straight back."

Lola chuckled in my ear. "You haven't done anything straight in your life, Spencer."

I pursed my lips together so I wouldn't smile, ended the call, and slid my phone in my pocket. Eli had gone back to the counter to give me what privacy the small foyer allowed, but he looked at me expectantly. "I'm sorry," I told him. "I have an issue back at work I need to sort out. Do you have a card I can take?"

He handed me his business card, and I told him I'd be in touch.

WHEN ANDREW CALLED me that night, I knew I had to tell him. "I saw Eli today."

There was only silence. Then, "You what?"

"I went into his work and made enquiries about tattoo posters I don't need."

It sounded like he changed the ear he had his phone to, then it sounded like he fidgeted. "Did you tell him who you were?"

"No, of course not."

"But he's seen you with me."

"I know." I tried to play it cool. "I'm not sure if he recognised me. He never let on."

"Jeez, Spencer. You could have blown the whole thing." He was obviously pissed with me, and probably rightfully so. "What did you do that for?"

"I was kind of hoping he did recognise me. I think he did, I'm not sure," I admitted. "But what I did was just pretty much guarantee us a reaction from him."

Truth be told, I was making things worse. I knew that. Eli was either going to push harder to get Andrew back, or he was not going to care at all. That selfish part of me was hoping for the latter.

And it had been a long time since I'd hoped for anything.

I was tempted to give him excuses and apologies, but I didn't. I needed him to speak first. It took eight long and heart-racing seconds. "And?" he asked.

"And what?"

"What did you think of him?"

I shrugged, even though he couldn't see. "He seemed nice."

"God, you really suck at lying." He huffed into the phone. "And considering you do it for a living, I would expect better."

"Ouch."

He laughed. "Well, it's true."

"I can lie convincingly to other people," I admitted. "Just not you. For some stupid reason."

I don't know how I knew, but I was pretty sure he was smiling. "Well, for that, you can buy dinner tomorrow night."

"Is that right?"

"Yes. Pizza and a movie. Seven o'clock."

"You're so bossy," I said. I'm surprised I could actually talk with how much I was grinning. "And anyway, how do you live on takeout and have the body you do?"

He laughed quietly. "I told you. I work out for an hour every morning before I go to work."

"Do you wear tight gym shorts and muscle tops? Because I would totally get out of bed to see that."

He chuckled into the phone. "See you tomorrow at seven."

"So you told Eli no to the date tomorrow night?"

"I told him I couldn't," he answered. He cleared his throat. "You know, treat 'em mean to keep 'em keen."

I couldn't stop the stupid smile on my face. "Oh, I'm sorry. I just was picturing you wearing tight gym shorts and a muscle top. What were you saying?"

He snorted. "Good night, Spencer." He disconnected the call, but I was still smiling at the mental images of Andrew in his gym clothes.

FRIDAY DRAGGED. Like *really* dragged. I helped Emilio and Daniela in the shop for a while, made arrangements for when and where to see my next client on Monday afternoon. I cleaned my apartment, I read, I ate, I did all those things, and then I spent a good few hours getting ready and picking out clothes while the clock ticked down like its battery was dying. Because I was losing my mind.

But, like a good boy, at seven o'clock, holding a pizza as requested, I knocked on Andrew's front door. I heard what sounded like him coming down the stairs, the rattle of the lock on the door, and then he swung the door inward and smiled.

And like some cosmic shift, time was good again. "Oh good," he said. "I'm starving."

"Hi, not bad. Yourself?" I joked at his complete lack of greeting. "Cab here was okay, but I don't think the cabbie appreciated the smell of pizza in his car."

Andrew laughed. "Sorry. Hi, how are you? That's good. How was your cab ride here?"

I handed him the pizza box. "You're welcome."

He walked through the living room, slid the pizza onto the table, and went straight into the kitchen. "Beer or soda?"

"Beer's good."

"Yes it is," he replied, came back out, and handed me one. He was wearing jeans and an old button-down shirt that looked well-worn and soft. Jesus. His feet were bare. I couldn't remember ever telling him that I found jeans and bare feet hot, but damn.

"They don't smell bad," he said, wiggling his toes. "Promise."

God help me. I totally got caught staring at his feet. When I glanced up at him, he took one look at my face and a slow smile spread across his lips. "Oh."

"Shut up."

He chuckled and clinked his beer bottle to mine. "So? Pizza? Or do you wanna stare at my feet a little longer?"

Ignoring him before I died of embarrassment, I rolled my eyes and sat at the table. I opened the box and took a slice. "So? Anyone at work giving you a hard time about the photo we posted on your Facebook?"

He almost bit into his first slice but stopped before it got to his mouth. He groaned. "It's been painful," he said. "All week." He took a mouthful and hummed appreciatively. "Mmm, this is good."

He devoured four slices to my two. "Didn't you eat today?" I asked.

He shook his head and washed his food down with a mouthful of beer. "Nope. I've been avoiding the lunchroom because, well, because the latest game around the department seems to be 'Let's ask Andrew 101 questions about his new boyfriend.'"

"New *boyfriend*, huh?" I smiled. I liked that way more than I should have. "What's he like? Bet he's handsome."

A rush of heat coloured his cheeks and crept down his neck. "Shut up. You know what I mean."

I picked at the label on my beer bottle. "I've been called worse things."

His smile faltered. "By jealous ex-boyfriends?"

"Actually, more by the client," I admitted. "The guy who I'm trying to help. Clearly I'm not their type, and they find my boredom at city gala openings or nights at the opera a little uncouth."

"Really? You had to go to gala openings and the opera?" He frowned. "And they belittled you for it?"

"You'd be surprised," I said softly. "They're paying me to

do a job, I guess. They treat me the same way they treat the people who dry clean their clothes or wash their car."

Andrew nodded slowly, and there was a brief look of hurt on his face before he replaced it with a tight smile. He cleared his throat. "You must think it's terribly boring to have a Friday night of pizza and a movie then." It wasn't a question. More like a confirmation to himself. "I'm not much into going out."

"Are you kidding me? This is perfect. Pizza and a movie is my kind of night. Sure, getting all frocked up in a suit is cool every now and then, but that shit gets old."

He smiled somewhat more genuinely, but it was still a little forced. "Frocked up?"

"You know, dressed up?" I shrugged. "I swear, everyone I know should take a lesson in Australianisms so I don't have to keep explaining these things."

"Or I could just book myself in for an elective lobotomy..."

I gaped at him. Literally. My mouth fell open. He roared laughing and put his foot up on the table. "Here, look at my bare foot."

"Fuck you."

That only made him laugh some more.

"You suck."

He waggled his eyebrows at me. "Yes. Yes I do."

I groaned, in part because his pun was lame, and in part because now I was thinking about him sucking dick.

"Shut up and put the movie on."

Still chuckling to himself, he took the pizza box into the kitchen, then he joined me in the living room. He handed me a full beer and was still smiling as he put the DVD in.

"What are we watching?" I asked. He tossed the cover to

me. It was *How to Train Your Dragon 2.* "Seriously? We're watching a cartoon?"

He stood up, looking honestly offended, his smile well and truly gone. "I um, well, I, we don't have to. I just thought…"

"Did you have that lobotomy already?" I asked with a smirk.

Now he glared. "You're an ass."

"Thank you."

He collected his beer from the coffee table and planted himself on the sofa, not right next to me, but not at the other end either. He stretched out his legs and put his feet on the coffee table as the movie began, so I did the same.

He cleared his throat. "Ah, are you alright there, making yourself at home?" He was staring at my shoes.

"Yes, thanks," I said with a grin, not taking my eyes off the television. I was pretty sure if I looked at him, I'd grab him by the face and kiss him until he came. *Fuck.* Now I was thinking about that. I swallowed hard. Jesus, the air in the room was suddenly heady and I could feel how close he was without looking. "So, um," I coughed and nodded toward the screen. "Which shots of this have you drawn?"

So as the movie played, Andrew told me about different scenes he'd done, what parts he liked, which were difficult, which were his favourite. But then something happened. In the movie. And it came from nowhere, and I wasn't expecting it. I had no clue and no time to prepare myself. It was a kid's movie for fuck's sake.

The father died.

In the movie. The father died. And a wave of memories and emotions hit me, like being crash-tackled from the blind-side. I certainly didn't see it coming.

I took some deep, quiet breaths, not wanting to draw attention to myself. I stared at the wall and realised I was staring at drawings from this very movie, and that didn't help at all. So then I stared at the top of the TV screen. There was writing about screen definition, and I stared so hard at it, trying to deliberately not watch the movie, that I must have stared too hard because my eyes started to water. I let out the slowest breath I could manage, but Andrew was too close, and he heard how shaky it was. He turned to me and started to laugh and was no doubt about to say something about crying in a kid's movie.

But then he saw my face.

He sat up and fumbled with the remote before clicking the whole TV off. I shot up off the sofa and went into the kitchen to catch my breath. *Oh, fuck.* The burn in my chest was as vivid now as it was years ago.

Andrew was right behind me. He put his hand on my arm. "Spencer, I'm sorry. I should've known... I gathered something had happened. I didn't even think about the dad."

I shook my head and put the heel of my hand against my sternum to counter the pain there. "It's okay. You weren't to know." I took another breath. "That just came from nowhere. I'm sorry."

He had a hand on either arm, his face was etched with worry. "Don't apologise. It's me who should be apologising. Your dad?"

I let my head fall back, and I let a shaky breath out at the ceiling. "My father..." Andrew moved his hands from my arms, but before he could take a step back, I snatched his t-shirt. I fisted the material, keeping him right where he was. I needed him to stay close. I wanted to tell him what happened. I wanted to tell him why the four blackbirds were tattooed on my arm, but I couldn't. I never spoke about them. I wore those inked reminders like armour, but I couldn't form the words.

"Do you want to talk about it?" he asked gently.

I shook my head.

"Okay," he said. "That's okay."

He put his hand to my face, and I leaned into it. I fucking leaned. And like he knew what I needed—what my heart and soul craved—he pulled me against him.

I'd never felt anything so good in my life. He was warm and strong, he was safe and right. I buried my face into his neck, and I might have held on a little too tight. But he smelled so perfect and his arms went around me like they were meant to do just that.

I didn't want to let go. I wanted to kiss his neck, I wanted to lift my face and kiss his lips. I wanted to know what he tasted like. I wanted him to hold me, and take me to bed, have his way with me.

And when I pulled back, he stayed right there. He looked into my eyes and licked his lips. He was going to kiss me...

Then my stupid hand was against his chest, keeping him at a safe non-kissing distance. *Fuck.* My head was swimming, my heart was hammering and aching, my stomach was in knots, and I was a fucking mess.

Then my stupid mouth said, "I should go."

He blinked and shook his head, as if startled from some kind of stupor. "Yeah." I stepped away, but he stopped me with a hand on my arm. "Spencer?"

I looked at him, fighting every fibre in my body that wanted to fall back into his arms, to kiss him.

He looked torn apart. "Are you sure you're okay?"

I nodded. "Yeah." *Of course I'm okay. I've been okay for years.* "I'll see you tomorrow. I'll come around four?" I didn't wait for him to answer. I turned and walked out as fast as my stupid feet would take me.

OF COURSE SLEEP didn't come easy. Hell, it barely came at all. I finally managed about two hours shut eye after the sun made its way over the horizon. The sound of screeching tires on the street below woke me up, and so I didn't lie around all day thinking about stuff I didn't want to be thinking about, I put on some running clothes and hit the pavement.

I ran all the way down to Venice Beach. It was a warm Saturday morning, so it was packed. There were people walking dogs, roller blading, cycling, jogging. Some looked a million dollars, some looked like they were doing the walk of shame. But the crowd, the smells, and the noise was every-thing I needed to distract me. I loved this place. It was actu-ally the first place I'd came to when I'd arrived in LA and, after doing the tourist thing of checking out Abbot Kinney Boulevard, I'd found myself looking through a tattoo shop window. I'd walked in and started chatting with the owner. He'd introduced himself as Emilio, and the rest is pretty much history.

It was Emilio who had done the four blackbird tattoos that now graced my right forearm. I'd come to America with just one shoulder inked. Emilio had helped me better than any therapist could have. There is something cathartic about having your scars inked into your skin.

Maybe that's what I needed. Another tattoo. Some pain on the outside to ease the pain on the inside. Yes, that's exactly what I needed.

With a new mission, I jogged back home. I hadn't run that far in a long time and my legs and lungs burned. The pain was welcome. I considered not going up to my apartment and just going straight in to see Emilio, but I knew he was busy and probably wouldn't have appreciated a sweaty me in his tattoo shop. As I made my way to the back stairs, Daniela and Lola were at the back door talking. It wasn't uncommon for them to sneak out the back and have a laugh or a bitch session or whatever it was they talked about.

"Hey," I said in greeting.

They both looked me up and down. Lola spoke first. "You okay, Spence?"

"Yeah, why wouldn't I be?"

"Um, you're running," Daniela answered.

"Needed to clear my head," I said, taking the stairs on shaky legs. I got to the top and turned around. They were both watching me. "You don't know if Emilio's got a free session today?"

Daniela shook her head. "I can find out for you. Who wants some work done?"

"Me."

They both just stood there, looking up at me. Neither said a word.

I opened my door. "I'll be down in a bit."

"What time are you meeting Andrew?" Lola asked.

"Four."

She looked at her watch. "Um..."

"What time is it?"

"Just after three."

"Shit. Where did today go?" I raced inside and went straight for a shower. By the time I was dressed and ready, I found Lola at the bottom of the stairs, waiting.

She looked me up and down. "Jesus, looking good Spence."

I flashed her a smile. "Thanks."

"Come on," she nodded to the car park. "I'll drive you."

I knew it was coming. I was actually surprised it took her three blocks. "Tonight's the big night, huh?"

"Yep."

"You okay?"

"Fine. Why?"

She looked at me for a beat too long. "Spence."

"I'm fine, Lolz," I said, knowing that name would stop her. She hated it. She pulled a face, and I pointed up ahead at where Lola needed to turn and gave a few directions. I used the break to change subjects. "How's Gabe's nipple piercing going?"

Her eyes sparked with mischief. "Oh, he likes it."

"He likes it, or you like it?"

"I like what it does to him."

That made me laugh. "That good, huh?"

"You should get one," she said, swerving in and out of lanes. "Actually, I'm surprised you don't have any piercings."

I gripped onto the dash, trying to sound like her driving didn't scare the bejeezus outta me. "Something I could work on, you reckon?"

She nodded enthusiastically. "You'll be surprised at how good they feel." Then she said, "You're thinking of getting more ink?"

"Yep. Just need to find the right piece."

"Cool." I knew she wanted to say more, but thankfully, she let it go.

"Just up here," I said, pointing to Andrew's place.

"Nice," she replied.

It really was. "Yeah."

"Look, Spencer," she said, pulling the car up to the kerb. "I know you've got a job to do here tonight, but I think if you talked to Andrew beforehand—"

"Lola, I'll be fine. Thank you for the lift."

And with that, I got out of Cindy Crawford and made my way up the path. I waved her off, pretending not to see the sadness on her face and pressed Andrew's intercom button. He opened the door and gave me a smile that made my heart trip over. Though he eyed me cautiously. "Hey," he said, letting me in. "You look great."

I had put on my best pants, a blue waistcoat that matched my shoes, and my white sleeves were rolled to my elbows. My hair was styled up, my beard trimmed, and I'd even put on some cologne because, well, smelling good was a man's secret weapon.

I didn't want him to feel bad about my freak out last night. Hell, I didn't even want him to mention it. "Get your laundry done today?"

He chuckled. "I did."

"And the gym?"

"Yep," he said, walking into the living room. "Am I that predictable?"

"No, not at all," I replied. He raised an eyebrow at me. "Okay, so maybe just a little."

His smile slid away, and he put his hand through his hair. I waited for it. He was going to say something like 'Look, about last night,' and it was the last thing I wanted to talk about, so I changed subjects completely. "Can you teach me to play something on your piano?"

My request stopped him, and he spun to look at his piano. "Oh. Um." He exhaled loudly. "Sure. I guess."

I walked over to the piano and sat on one end of the bench seat. It really was a beautiful piece of furniture, instrument, whatever. Not that I was any kind of expert in grand pianos or anything, but it really was special.

Andrew sat beside me, our thighs and arms pressed

together, and he lifted the lid. "Have you played anything before?"

"On the piano? No. God, I struggled with the triangle."

He smiled at that. "That surprises me. I would have thought with how musically inclined you are, that you could play *something*."

"I can," I said proudly. "I can play records."

Andrew chuckled and put his fingers to the keys. He explained the chords and octaves, but lost me when he added in the black keys, and if I was being truly honest, I started thinking about how long and elegant his fingers were and how they'd feel on my skin… Damn, I bet he could play me like a song.

"Spencer?"

"Oh. Sorry. Got side tracked by your fingers."

He chuckled. "Put your fingers like this, right index on F."

I did that, then he lifted my hands and moved them down a few keys. "Oh, *that* F."

His shoulders shook as he laughed, and he taught me which keys were which, and we were soon playing the most masterful *Chopsticks* ever played. Well, to me it was. Andrew probably last played it when he was four.

I gave up in the end, declaring myself *pianocally* challenged.

"That is not a word."

"Yes it is." I grinned. "Play me something."

"What?"

"Play me something. Anything. Your favourite," I said. "*Moonlight Sonata* or whatever it was called."

He looked back at the keys, then to me. "You sure?"

"Absolutely."

So he did. And oh my God. I've never heard anything so beautiful. Ever. He closed his eyes and he lost himself in each note. He didn't need sheet music to read from; he knew it by heart. It was perfection.

The last note hung in the air like some ethereal entity. His hands fell to his lap, and he finally looked at me, all vulnerable, like he'd shown a part of himself to me not many people ever got to see.

I should have given him some intelligent accolade, but all I could manage was, "Wow."

He let out a nervous breath, his lips curled into a smile. "You liked it?"

"Loved it. Now play me one of your jazz-funk songs." Then remembering my manners, I tacked on, "Please."

His whole demeanour changed. His eyes sparked with light and his smile was a cheeky one. He put his hands to the keys and played the funkiest piano solo I'd ever heard. I could picture people from the 20s dancing in some swinging jazz bar to this song. His whole body moved when he played; he put all of himself into the music. It was easy to tell this was what he loved. Sure, he played Beethoven like he respected it. But this, he played jazz because he loved it.

When the song finished, all I could do was sigh. "I could listen to you play all day long."

"Really?"

"Hell yes. Why does that surprise you?"

He shrugged. "It's just that it used to bug Eli."

I stared at him. "It what?"

"Bugged him. If he was reading or whatever. I guess it's loud and annoying." He made a face. "I used to play when he was asleep."

I couldn't believe it. The more he told me about Eli, the more I wanted to punch him in the throat. "Was he crazy? You playing the piano is like my most favourite thing."

Andrew's cheeks heated to a beautiful pink. "Oh. Thanks."

I shook my head. "I can't believe he would say that. What a wanker."

Andrew looked down the keyboard and never replied.

"Sorry, that was out of line," I said quietly. I was sorry I was out of line. I didn't say it because I was wrong.

Andrew stood up from the piano. "Well, I should probably go take a shower and get ready," he said. "Do you mind? I was going to shower earlier but lost track of time."

"No, it's fine." Whether he was going to shower now just to freshen up or to jerk off, I wasn't sure. I hoped for the latter then had to stop the mental images that caused my dick to stir. Then I spotted his laptop. "Hey, can I borrow your computer for a minute?"

"Sure. Help yourself."

"Can I check your Facebook? I want to see what Eli's been up to."

He blinked. "Um. Oh, okay. I guess." He shrugged one shoulder. "Just don't comment or private message anyone pretending to be me. Don't get into any conversations with my mother, and don't invite my sister over for dinner."

I laughed. "Deal."

Andrew went upstairs, and I took his laptop to the sofa. I wanted to check out Facebook to see what comments were on the photo we'd uploaded but didn't want to without his okaying it first. So I decided to see what I could dig up on Eli.

The guy was a douche, and what Andrew ever saw in him, I couldn't even guess. Maybe he was hung. Maybe Andrew had a thing for guys with big dicks. *Well, he should like me just fine.* I snorted and looked around the room like someone might have seen me.

Andrew had a few comments and notifications, which I

ignored. None were from Eli, so they weren't any of my business. I searched up Eli and scrolled through his timeline until I found some photos. With the help of a right-click and 'search Google' prompt, I was trawling the web for dirt on Eli.

Nothing out of the ordinary came up. Even with an image search and using the location feature, nothing weird showed up. From what I could gather from my ten minutes with Detective Google, he wasn't leading some double life or anything creepy or sinister. He was disappointingly normal. Still a douche, but a disappointingly normal douche.

Going back to a general web search, I typed his place of employment in, along with his name, and used keywords like education, degree, and address. And it really was shocking what information was readily available on the Internet.

Eli Masterson had applied for a job at Fujifilm in the graphics department. I didn't know exactly what he did at his printing job and maybe it wasn't such a stretch to move from one to the other, but I had to wonder if Andrew knew.

Did Andrew suggest it? Did Andrew try and get him the job?

"So," I hedged when he came back downstairs. I ignored how good he smelled and how he looked even better with wet hair. "How did you start working at DreamWorks?"

He seemed surprised by my question. "Um, I got my Bachelor of Fine Arts in Character Animation. When I was doing my Masters in Experimental Animation, I actually worked with them as part of my internship."

"Oh, so it's incredibly difficult," I said, rather stupidly. "All you had to say is 'you need to be the best in the industry'."

He smiled at that. "Why?"

"No reason exactly," I said. "What degrees did Eli have?"

Andrew's eyebrows narrowed. "Why?"

"I'm just wondering why he would have applied for a job at Fujifilm, that's all," I told him. "Was he qualified?"

Andrew stared at me in a way that told me, in no uncertain terms, he knew nothing of the job application. "What?"

"Was he a cartoonographer as well?" I asked. "Or maybe he applied for a different division? Something else entirely, maybe?"

He shook his head slowly. "He wanted to do..." He stopped talking. "What do you mean he applied for a job there? When?"

"It only gives the date of publication. Three months ago." I turned the laptop on my knees so he could see the screen. "But it's got his name and your address, so it was when he was living here."

He took a few tentative steps over, then sat beside me. He never took his eyes off the screen. I handed him the laptop and he read the information I'd found. Admittedly it wasn't much, but it was clearly news to Andrew.

After a long, silent minute, he asked, "What does that mean?"

"I don't know."

"Fujifilm have just opened a 3D art division at Universal Studios in Singapore," he said, brows knitted together. He shook his head. "He doesn't even have a portfolio for that kind of application. Even in the printing industry, he'd need examples of his work."

"Andrew," I said gently. "I don't know much about how these things, but did he have access to your work?"

He stared at me, his eyes wide and vulnerable, and the colour drained from his face. "Oh no." He bolted off the sofa and took the stairs two at a time. I followed him as he ran into his closet and he pulled his favourite print off the wall. He turned it over and clawed at the back of the frame, lifting those annoying little metal tabs until he pulled the back of the frame out. He was looking for something. He sighed, pure relief, and held it up. His signature was clearly there, even the ink bleed on the canvas. It was the original.

Then he took another one off the wall, so I did too, and one by one we opened each frame. By the time they'd all been checked, we were sitting on the floor in his closet surrounded by drawing boards and empty frames. Andrew leaned against the wall and sighed. "These are all original," he said. Though we both knew Eli worked at a printing company. The lady he worked with even said he specialized in framed prints.

Then his eyes went wide. "My dragons," he mumbled and scampered to his feet.

Oh hell no.

He ran back downstairs and into the living room. He stopped in front of the three framed drawings, like he couldn't bear to know if those weren't his originals.

"I'll check them," I told him. I gently lifted the first frame off the wall and laid it facedown on his dining table. I undid the metal tabs and pulled the backing off, and there in all its original glory was Andrew's signature. "It's yours," I whispered.

He visibly sagged and put his hand to his heart. "Oh, thank god."

I checked the other two, and they were the original pieces. "Andrew," I hedged. "He could have copied them."

"He'd need original pieces for authentication," he said. He put his hands to his forehead and barked out a laugh. "God, I almost panicked."

"Almost?" I asked. If that was almost, I'd hate to see a full-on panic. "I was ready to kill him."

He laughed, his relief clearly evident. "I feel kinda bad now for doubting him."

"Andrew," I said softly. Cautiously. "It doesn't change the fact he applied for a job in another country while he was living here and didn't even tell you."

He looked like I'd slapped him. It took him a while to answer. "Eli might be a lot of things, but he's not a thief."

And there it was. He was still defending him, even if he'd thought him capable of stealing just a minute ago. A reminder that he had feelings for him, and I was fucking delusional to think otherwise.

I strangled down my emotions and put on my best front. "Okay," I swallowed hard. "We better get these all put back together before we head out. Dinner first? I'm kind of hungry."

He stared at me for the longest moment. "Yeah. Of course."

NINE

BY THE TIME WE'D LEFT THE RESTAURANT, I WAS ready for this to be over. I tried not to read too much into the way he questioned the waiter on shellfish allergy precautions taken when cooking on my behalf or the way we talked for almost two hours straight without the slightest lull in conversation.

We never mentioned Eli, and that was more than fine with me.

I really needed this to be finished. I needed Eli to either want Andrew back or to walk away for good. As much as I didn't want it to be over, it was doing my head in. And my heart.

I had to put these foolish feelings aside and concentrate on my job.

The bar was already busy. The jazz music had the crowd buzzed. It was a great spot, and I made a mental note to come back here when Andrew was no longer in my life.

I bought us a drink and found us a tall table, though it was crowded and there wasn't much room, so we were standing pretty close. Andrew had his back to the crowd, so I could see over his shoulder if Eli decided to show.

And of course he did. I knew he would. We'd baited him, hook, line, and sinker. I put my hand on Andrew's waist and leaned right in to speak into his ear. "He's here."

Eli made his way to the bar, but he was scanning the room. It didn't take him long to spot us. His eyes were narrowed and stormy, his jaw was set. He was clearly not very happy with me being so close to Andrew. Maybe he recognised me. I didn't know. I didn't care.

And then foolish pride and wishful thinking made me take it one step further. I figured this was it. This was the first and last chance I'd have to do this, my one chance to know if he tasted as good as I knew he would. I stepped right in close, pinning Andrew against the table so Eli would have a side-on view. I put one hand on his chest and leaned in to whisper in his ear. "Don't look, but he's watching us." I pulled back and put my fingers under his chin. "Can I kiss you?"

Andrew's eyes went wide, his breath caught, and he nodded. So I softly pressed my lips to his, feeling the warmth of his lips. It was heady, and my stupid heart was hammering. I knew I shouldn't want more, but my head spun, and pure desire threw caution and reason out the window. My stupid brain was nowhere to be found. I slid my hand along his jaw and tilted his face to mine, and I kissed him properly.

He was soft lips and warm breath, bourbon and everything I wanted. This kiss wasn't for show. It wasn't a part of my deal to make his ex jealous; this was me, kissing him because I wanted him. I had feelings for him, confused and frightening feelings that I couldn't begin to understand.

I was kissing him. Open mouthed, eager lips and tasting tongues. And he was kissing me back. He slid one hand around my back and pulled me closer, the other around my neck. And fuck, he could kiss.

When we slowed and pulled apart, his eyes were unfocused, his lips a little flushed. He looked kiss-drunk and smug.

It was a perfect kiss. He was everything right for me. If a person was designed just for me, to be the yin to my yang, it was Andrew.

Yet, I'd just broken every personal and professional rule I'd ever set for myself. I'd failed not only myself, but Andrew too. He was paying me to provide a service, and I'd crossed the line.

"Uh, wow," Andrew said breathily. He licked his lips. "God, you can kiss."

"Not bad yourself," I said, trying to joke, but the ache in my chest made it impossible to pull off. I took a breath to collect myself and be the professional he needed me to be. We'd somehow changed places, and I now had my back to the bar. "Did Eli see that?"

"Oh," he recoiled and looked over my shoulder. "Um, he's gone."

My heart soared. Usually if they didn't confront us, it meant the relationship was really over. And that shouldn't have made me happy. That was the wrong outcome for Andrew. I was so conflicted. My head was a mess, my heart, well, I'd deal with that later. "Andrew, if he's gone..." And I couldn't do it. I didn't want to give him the bad news. I didn't want to hurt him, but it would also mean my job with him was done. I wanted to ask him if what I felt was real, I wanted to ask him if he felt it too. Surely, he did. It couldn't just be one-sided. "Let's go, hey?"

He frowned but nodded, and I took his hand and led us

through the crowded bar. We were almost to the door when someone grabbed Andrew's arm.

Eli.

Fuck. Fuck, fuck, fucking fuck.

Eli glanced at me, then back to Andrew. "Can we talk?"

And there it was. My heart squeezed, and the hope that had been there just a moment ago, was snuffed out. This was mission accomplished. Eli wanted Andrew back. Andrew got what he wanted, what he paid me for.

Andrew glanced at me, like he was unsure of what to do. I could see it in his eyes. *Is this part of the plan? What do I say? How do I act?* He was looking at me to take the lead. What I wanted to do was tell Eli to get his hand off Andrew and fuck off.

But I couldn't. That's not what Andrew had hired me to do. I forced a smile on my face, and as much as it killed me, I said, "I'll just wait outside."

I turned and made my way out of the bar, blood pounding in my ears, my heart hammering and my stomach turning. I just needed air. I needed to leave.

How could one night be the very best and the very worst?

I didn't wait. I kept on walking.

I'll just wait outside, I'd said. Code for good luck.

Oh God, I thought I was gonna puke.

A few blocks later I came up to a liquor store and went in. One bottle of Maker's Mark later, and I headed for home. I needed to drown my sorrows, and I needed to forget. I needed to kill whatever stupid hope I'd had, to convince myself I wasn't falling for him.

By the time I saw the neon lights of the tattoo shop, I was drunk. Really fucking drunk. Emilio sometimes worked late, and I was glad to see the lights were still on in the shop. I pushed the door open and tripped up the step, stumbling into the store. "Fuck man, 'Milio, need to fix your step."

Emilio, who was just finishing up an ink job, stood up. He patted his client and said, "Hang on one minute," pulled off his glove, and walked over to me. "Daniela!"

Daniela came out from the back, and I tried not to notice how she frowned when she saw me. I held up the now half-empty bottle of bourbon. "Drink?"

Emilio ignored me. Instead he spoke to Daniela. "Call Lola." Daniela disappeared again, and I turned to face Emilio, but the floor tilted and I swayed. Emilio caught me. "What happened?" he asked.

"Andrew," I started. "Eli..." And I had to wipe my stupid cheeks because stupid tears fell out of my stupid fucking eyes.

"Oh, man," Emilio mumbled.

"I thought he was different," I slurred.

"So did I," Emilio said.

I sucked back a ragged breath and my voice cracked. "What's wrong with me?"

He pulled me against him. "Nothing, man. Not one thing."

Daniela came out. "She's on her way."

Then I felt worse than I already did. "She didn't need to come."

Daniela put her arm around me. "Come with me," she said quietly and led me to one of the back cubicles. She offered me a chair, but I opted for the floor instead. I leaned back against the wall, and she kneeled in front of me and put her hand to my face. "There's nothing wrong with you, Spencer. Not one thing."

"Why did he...?" I shook my head. I knew the answer to that. "So fucking stupid. I knew he was in love with someone else. That's why he came to me, to help get him back, and just so happens I'm really fucking good at my job."

Daniela put her hand to my face. "Oh, Spencer, honey." She looked so sad, and I couldn't bear it. I drank more bourbon instead.

It wasn't long after that Daniela was gone and it was Lola in front of me. She was trying to catch her breath, like she'd ran the whole way here. I thought I had a handle on my stupid emotions, and I did, until I saw the sadness on her face. "Tell me what happened," she said.

"I kissed him," I told her. My words were slow and slurred. "Not some ploy, not some strategy. It was me, kissing him."

"What did he do?"

"He kissed me back. It was, God, it was the best kiss I've ever had." I could still feel the warmth of his lips, the taste of his tongue...

"Then what happened?"

"I kinda panicked and said we should leave, and Eli—fucking Eli—stopped us on the way out." I took another mouthful of bourbon. Lola took the bottle off me. I didn't protest. I had to look away from Gabe, who was leaning against the door, looking back at me with the saddest fucking look on his face. I focused on Lola instead. "And I let him go. I fucking let him go." I couldn't stop the tears again. "Thought he was different."

"Oh, hun."

"And I'm losing my shit," I said, wiping my stupid tears with the back of my hand. "And it hurts."

"Because you're falling in love with him," Lola whispered.

Then there were other voices and Gabe walked away from the door, but my booze infused mind was stuck on what Lola said. I stared at her, but I couldn't bear the pity in her eyes, so I looked away and stared at the wall instead. I tried to find the words to deny it but couldn't. It was never supposed to get to this. I was never supposed to fall in love. More stupid tears came, and I dug the heels of my hands into my eyes. "Stupid fucking tears."

She squeezed my arm.

"You know why I do what I do?" I asked, looking at her. My words were thick with tears. "Emotional detachment. Distance and separation. And no one can tell me they don't want me."

And there it was.

It always came back to that.

No one can tell me they don't want me.

"Oh, Spencer," Lola whispered. Her eyes welled with tears. "Andrew's not like your family."

I shook my head and breathed in deep, trying to get a fucking grip. It didn't work. "He didn't want me either," I said with a wave of fresh tears.

The room started to spin a little and it took a while for my stupid brain to realise Andrew was standing in front of me. His eyes were wide, no doubt the sight of me losing my shit on the floor was a shock to him. He'd obviously just heard what Lola said about my family. I wiped at my stupid fucking tears, just as Lola turned to see who I was looking at. She stood up and went to him, whispering something I couldn't hear. I pulled my knees up and dug the heels of my hands into my eyes again.

When I looked up, I was expecting him to be gone. I was expecting him to have bailed, fled the ball of crazy, sitting drunk, crying on the floor. But he didn't. He picked up the bottle of bourbon and sat his arse down next to me. Instead of telling me I was stupid, instead of telling me I was unwanted, he put the bottle to his mouth and took a swig. He hissed at the burn.

"Andrew," I tried to say, but my voice cracked.

He slid his hand over mine and held it tight. "It's okay."

I shook my head. "Eli?"

"Eli's gone."

Oh God. "S'my fault. I fucked up. Sorry."

He took another mouthful of bourbon and squeezed my hand. "No. You didn't. He did. But I'm glad," he said. "Because of him, I met you."

My heart hammered and he was saying all the right words, and he hadn't run a mile when he saw me, like it meant maybe I had a chance. It brought fresh tears to my eyes. "I'm a mess."

He threaded his fingers with mine. "I can see that."

I hung my head. Tired, drunk, and an emotional fucking wreck. "You saw through all my bullshit," I told him. I held out our joined hands and pointed to the blackbirds on my arm. "And these. No one has ever..." I shook my head and swallowed back new tears. "This one is my dad." I pointed to the biggest. Then to the other three in turn. "My mum, my two brothers."

He ran his other hand over my arm, as though his touch could heal the pain there.

"They're not really dead," I whispered. "Well, they are to me. That's what my father said, the last thing he said to me was that I was dead to them."

"Oh, Spencer."

I let the tears fall. I didn't even try to stop them. "I was sixteen," I choked out. "And gay."

He let go of my hand so he could put his arm around me, and he pulled me against him. That warm, safe place I hadn't felt in years. "N'then there was you," I mumbled.

He kissed the top of my head. "And then there was you."

TEN

I WOKE UP TO AN UNGODLY PAIN IN MY HEAD. THE blinds were letting in piercing sunlight, my stomach rolled, and then I remembered...

Kissing Andrew, leaving him at the bar with Eli, drinking half a bottle of bourbon, being a fucking mess in front of everyone, Andrew coming back to me.

He came back to me.

I had no recollection of getting up to my apartment. I remembered the looks of worry on Emilio and Daniela's faces. Lola, how she tried to help me. Then I remembered Andrew sitting down on the floor next to me.

I sat up, then really wished I hadn't. "Hello?" I croaked out.

Silence. Ugh. My head hurt.

I went to grab my phone to check for the time, but there was a piece of paper on top of it. It was a hand-written note. "Come downstairs."

It wasn't Emilio's handwriting, it wasn't Daniela's or Lola's, not even Gabe's. It was Andrew's.

I shot out of bed, then had to steady myself on the wall.

Ugh. Stupid hangovers. I made it to the bathroom, where I noticed I was still dressed from last night. Though someone had taken my shoes off. The shower was heaven, and I scrubbed the stench of bourbon from my skin. Brushing my teeth made me feel almost human, but I couldn't stay in there for long.

Andrew was waiting for me in Emilio's shop.

I got dressed and only stopped to pop some Advil before I went downstairs. Not even the retina-burning sunlight could slow me down. Gabe was at the back door, sucking on a filthy cigarette. The smell made me wanna hurl. He smiled. "Hey. How's your head?"

"Not great. Look, I'm really sorry about last night."

"Don't be," he said with a smile. "Someone's still here." He gave a nod to inside. "Spent the night on your couch apparently."

I tried not to smile, and without a word Gabe pushed the door with his foot, letting me in. "Thanks."

I didn't mean to intrude on private conversations, but Emilio, Daniela, Lola, and Andrew obviously weren't expecting me to come through the back door. I heard the tail end of them talking as I walked in. It was Emilio's voice. "... when his brother turned up, he was a mess."

My heart sank, and my already fragile stomach rolled. I guessed after my meltdown last night it was only fair that I would be their topic of conversation.

"That's when he got the birds tattooed on his arm?" Andrew asked.

"Yeah," Emilio answered. "They symbolize life after death. You know, new beginning, that kind of thing."

I walked out and Emilio saw me first. "Here he is! Feeling okay?"

"Like shit actually," I answered, but I couldn't take my eyes off Andrew. He was wearing my clothes.

He stood up slowly, smiling warily. "I uh, I had to borrow a shirt. I hope you don't mind?"

I shook my head. "Not at all."

And for the longest moment, we just stared at each other.

"Right then," Lola said, breaking me out of my stupor. "We'll just be out back." She grabbed Daniela's arm and left, dragging Emilio with them.

Then it was just me and him. I smiled. "Hey."

"Hey."

"You stayed."

"I did."

"I'm really sorry about last night."

"Don't apologise."

"I don't remember much," I admitted. "I remember losing my shit, which I can only apologise for. I'm not a basket case, I promise."

He walked over to me and stood within touching distance. "You hungry?" he asked. "We could grab a Moroccan breakfast?"

"Sounds perfect."

"We need to talk."

I nodded. "We do." I took a deep breath and asked the question I wasn't sure I wanted the answer to. "You spoke to Eli last night?"

He nodded. "I asked him about the prints and the job application. He admitted to making copies but couldn't bring himself to take the originals. He didn't even make the first round of interviews for that job because he didn't submit artwork. He said he was sorry."

I swallowed hard. "What did you tell him?"

"I told him it was over," Andrew said, staring right at me.

My heart thumped in my chest. "Is that right?"

A faint blush crept down his neck. "Yeah, I told him there was this Australian guy who knew more about me in two days than he did in eight months."

I gave him a breathy smile as relief coursed through me. "Is that right?"

Andrew put his hand to my face. "He gets me, like no one else has."

I nodded. "I know."

"And I was hoping he'd like to maybe get to know me a little better," he whispered.

I leaned into his hand and closed my eyes. "He does."

"I know he has some family issues," Andrew said quietly. "But that doesn't scare me." Not sure I could trust my voice to speak, I nodded, but he lifted my face. "Look at me," he whispered. I did as he asked, and there was only strength and honesty in his eyes. "It doesn't scare me, Spencer. In fact, I think you're something wonderful."

I swallowed down my emotions and ignored my hammering heart. "I think you're kinda great too."

I could feel his body heat, how close he was, his breath on my lips. His voice was a gruff whisper. "Can I kiss you?"

He was *right* there, so close, and all I could do was nod. My heart was beating triple time. Then he pressed his lips to mine. He held my face, so gently, and I put my hands around his waist. It was a sweet kiss, a kiss with promise. An *everything* kind of kiss.

It would have been perfect if Lola hadn't squealed from one of the cubicles. We broke apart with a nervous, relieved laugh.

"Sorry," she squeaked. She raced out and gave us both a quick hug. "I'm just so excited!" she cried, her hands to her mouth, before she ran back to the cubicle.

I couldn't help but laugh, and Andrew pulled me closer. The both of us were a bit embarrassed. He kissed me again, just real quick. "Come on. I'm starving," he said, taking my hand. He walked to the door. "You ready?"

I stopped. *Was I ready? To take this one step further? To finally let someone in? To tell him the story of Spencer Cohen and hope that he would still want me?*

With my heart in my mouth, I nodded. "Yeah. I'm ready."

~The End

ABOUT THE AUTHOR

N.R. Walker is an Australian author, who loves her genre of gay romance. She loves writing and spends far too much time doing it, but wouldn't have it any other way.

She is many things: a mother, a wife, a sister, a writer. She has pretty, pretty boys who live in her head, who don't let her sleep at night unless she gives them life with words.

She likes it when they do dirty, dirty things… but likes it even more when they fall in love.

She used to think having people in her head talking to her was weird, until one day she happened across other writers who told her it was normal.

She's been writing ever since…

ALSO BY N.R. WALKER

Blind Faith

Through These Eyes (Blind Faith #2)

Blindside: Mark's Story (Blind Faith #3)

Ten in the Bin

Gay Sex Club Stories 1

Gay Sex Club Stories 2

Point of No Return – Turning Point #1

Breaking Point – Turning Point #2

Starting Point – Turning Point #3

Element of Retrofit – Thomas Elkin Series #1

Clarity of Lines – Thomas Elkin Series #2

Sense of Place – Thomas Elkin Series #3

Taxes and TARDIS

Three's Company

Red Dirt Heart

Red Dirt Heart 2

Red Dirt Heart 3

Red Dirt Heart 4

Red Dirt Christmas

Cronin's Key

Cronin's Key II

Cronin's Key III

Cronin's Key IV - Kennard's Story

Exchange of Hearts

The Spencer Cohen Series, Book One

The Spencer Cohen Series, Book Two

The Spencer Cohen Series, Book Three

The Spencer Cohen Series, Yanni's Story

Blood & Milk

The Weight Of It All

A Very Henry Christmas (The Weight of It All 1.5)

Perfect Catch

Switched

Imago

Imagines

Imagoes

Red Dirt Heart Imago

On Davis Row

Finders Keepers

Evolved

Galaxies and Oceans

Private Charter

Nova Praetorian

A Soldier's Wish

Upside Down

The Hate You Drink

Sir

Tallowwood

Reindeer Games

The Dichotomy of Angels

Throwing Hearts

Pieces of You - Missing Pieces #1

Pieces of Me - Missing Pieces #2

Pieces of Us - Missing Pieces #3

Lacuna

Tic-Tac-Mistletoe

Bossy

Code Red

Dearest Milton James

Dearest Malachi Keogh

Christmas Wish List

Code Blue

Davo

The Kite

Learning Curve

Merry Christmas Cupid

To the Moon and Back

TITLES IN AUDIO:

Cronin's Key

Cronin's Key II

Cronin's Key III

Red Dirt Heart

Red Dirt Heart 2

Red Dirt Heart 3

Red Dirt Heart 4

The Weight Of It All

The Hate You Drink

Pieces of You

Pieces of Me

Pieces of Us

Tic-Tac-Mistletoe

Lacuna

Bossy

Code Red

Learning to Feel

Dearest Milton James

Dearest Malachi Keogh

Three's Company

Christmas Wish List

Code Blue

Davo

The Kite

Learning Curve

Merry Christmas Cupid

SERIES COLLECTIONS:

Red Dirt Heart Series

Turning Point Series

Thomas Elkin Series

Spencer Cohen Series

Imago Series

Blind Faith Series

FREE READS:

Sixty Five Hours

Learning to Feel

His Grandfather's Watch (And The Story of Billy and Hale)

The Twelfth of Never (Blind Faith 3.5)

Twelve Days of Christmas (Sixty Five Hours Christmas)

Best of Both Worlds

TRANSLATED TITLES:

ITALIAN

Fiducia Cieca (Blind Faith)

Attraverso Questi Occhi (Through These Eyes)

Preso alla Sprovvista (Blindside)

Il giorno del Mai (Blind Faith 3.5)

Cuore di Terra Rossa Serie (Red Dirt Heart Series)

Natale di terra rossa (Red dirt Christmas)

Intervento di Retrofit (Elements of Retrofit)

A Chiare Linee (Clarity of Lines)

Senso D'appartenenza (Sense of Place)

Spencer Cohen Serie (including Yanni's Story)

Punto di non Ritorno (Point of No Return)

Punto di Rottura (Breaking Point)

Punto di Partenza (Starting Point)

Imago (Imago)

Il desiderio di un soldato (A Soldier's Wish)

Scambiato (Switched)

Galassie e Oceani (Galaxies and Oceans)

FRENCH

Confiance Aveugle (Blind Faith)

A travers ces yeux: Confiance Aveugle 2 (Through These Eyes)

Aveugle: Confiance Aveugle 3 (Blindside)

À Jamais (Blind Faith 3.5)

Cronin's Key Series

Au Coeur de Sutton Station (Red Dirt Heart)

Partir ou rester (Red Dirt Heart 2)

Faire Face (Red Dirt Heart 3)

Trouver sa Place (Red Dirt Heart 4)

Le Poids de Sentiments (The Weight of It All)

Un Noël à la sauce Henry (A Very Henry Christmas)

Une vie à Refaire (Switched)

Evolution (Evolved)

Galaxies & Océans

Qui Trouve, Garde (Finders Keepers)

Sens Dessus Dessous (Upside Down)

Spencer Cohen Series

GERMAN

Flammende Erde (Red Dirt Heart)

Lodernde Erde (Red Dirt Heart 2)

Sengende Erde (Red Dirt Heart 3)

Ungezähmte Erde (Red Dirt Heart 4)

Vier Pfoten und ein bisschen Zufall (Finders Keepers)

Ein Kleines bisschen Versuchung (The Weight of It All)

Ein Kleines Bisschen Fur Immer (A Very Henry Christmas)

Weil Leibe uns immer Bliebt (Switched)

Drei Herzen eine Leibe (Three's Company)

Über uns die Sterne, zwischen uns die Liebe (Galaxies and Oceans)

Unnahbares Herz (Blind Faith 1)

Sehendes Herz (Blind Faith 2)

Hoffnungsvolles Herz (Blind Faith 3)

Verträumtes Herz (Blind Faith 3.5)

Thomas Elkin: Verlangen in neuem Design

Traummann töpfern leicht gemacht (Throwing Hearts)

THAI

Sixty Five Hours (Thai translation)

Finders Keepers (Thai translation)

SPANISH

Sesenta y Cinco Horas (Sixty Five Hours)

Los Doce Días de Navidad

Código Rojo (Code Red)

Código Azul (Code Blue)

Queridísimo Milton James

Queridísimo Malachi Keogh

El Peso de Todo (The Weight of it All)

Tres Muérdagos en Raya: Serie Navidad en Hartbridge

Lista De Deseos Navideños: Serie Navidad en Hartbridge

Spencer Cohen Libro Uno

Spencer Cohen Libro Dos

Spencer Cohen Libro Tres

La Historia de Yanni

Davo

Feliz Navidad Cupido: Serie Navidad en Hartbridge

CHINESE

Blind Faith